Bought partly with the book-token from the
Edinburgh Latin verse contest, which I won, on
11/10/77, from the Citizen bookshop in
St. Andrews, by

Helen Scott.

THE INVISIBLE MAN

HERBERT GEORGE WELLS
1866-1946

THE INVISIBLE MAN

H. G. WELLS

With an Introduction by

FRANK WELLS

COLLINS
LONDON AND GLASGOW

GENERAL EDITOR: G. F. MAINE

First published, 1897
This edition, 1953
Latest reprint, 1973

Printed in Great Britain
by Collins Clear-Type Press

HERBERT GEORGE WELLS

HERBERT GEORGE WELLS was born on September 21st, 1866 at Bromley, Kent. Destined for the profession of a draper, he became instead one of the great intellectual lights of his age.

His father, Joseph Wells, kept a small hardware shop and was an enthusiastic professional cricketer. His mother, whose maiden name was Neal, had been in domestic service before her marriage. The shop in Bromley High Street never prospered; its income was barely sufficient to keep the family above the poverty line.

From his father, young Herbert George ('Bertie' as he was called) had inherited a taste for reading which he was able to indulge freely at the local Literary Institute and lending library. He was sent to school locally, first to some cottage school and later to an establishment called Morley's Academy. In 1880, when the family found itself in great financial difficulties, Mrs. Wells was offered and accepted a post as housekeeper to her former employers at Uppark, Sussex, and Herbert George was apprenticed to a firm of drapers in Windsor. However, he did not satisfy his employers and had to leave after one month. For a very brief spell he acted as pupil teacher at a school in Somerset, and after that he was a chemist's assistant at Midhurst for one month (January 1881). In April of the same year he found himself once more a draper's apprentice, this time at Southsea. After two years in this soul-destroying occupation he could bear it no longer and left.

He next obtained a post as assistant master at Midhurst Grammar School, and in 1884 was awarded a scholarship (of one guinea a week) at the Normal School of Science (now the Imperial College of Science), South Kensington, London. For three years he studied physics, chemistry, geology, astronomy and biology—the latter under Professor Thomas H. Huxley. On termination of his studies he became assistant master in a school at Holt, North Wales. There he had a severe football accident from the effects of which he suffered for very many years. He returned to London in July 1888, and early in 1889 joined the staff of Henley House School at Kilburn. In October, 1890 he took a B.Sc. degree with first-class honours in zoology at London University. His next appointment (from 1891-93) was that of a biology tutor for the University Correspondence College.

In the summer of 1893 a serious hæmorrhage of the lungs forced him to take a long rest and to adopt a completely sedentary occupation. Around 1891-92 he had contributed essays to various educational and other journals and in 1893 while he was recuperating from his illness he began to write short stories, essays and reviews for periodicals and magazines, among them *The Pall Mall Gazette*, *St. James's Gazette*, *Black and White*, the *New Review* and *The Saturday Review*. In 1893 his first major work *A Textbook of Biology* was published. The year 1895 saw the publication of a volume of short stories (*The Stolen Bacillus*), a volume of collected essays, and of two novels, *The Time Machine* and *The Wonderful Visit*. The former established his reputation as a writer of extraordinary power and imagination.

In 1895 also he married Miss Amy Catherine Robbins, a former pupil of his—his first marriage (1891) to a cousin having meanwhile been dissolved. Two sons were subsequently born of his second marriage (George Philip, 1901, and Frank, 1903). The next few years brought his series of great scientific romances: *The Island of Dr. Moreau* (1896), *The Invisible Man* (1897), *The War of the Worlds* (1898), *The First Men in the Moon* (1901), as well as many short stories, articles and novels, among them *Love and Mr. Lewisham* (1901).

In 1900 Wells built himself a house at Sandgate near Folkestone, which remained his home for nearly a decade, in the course of which he rose to a position of world-wide literary fame. There, at Sandgate, he wrote some of his most celebrated works, e.g. *Anticipations*, a volume of essays on sociological problems (1901), *The Sea Lady* (1902), *The Food of the Gods* (1904), *Kipps*, *A Modern Utopia* (both in 1905), *In the Days of the Comet* (1906), *The War in the Air* (1908), *Tono Bungay*, *Anne Veronica* (both in 1909), and *The History of Mr. Polly* (1910).

At the turn of the century, his health having greatly improved, Wells began to make frequent trips to the European Continent and in 1906 he went on his first tour to the United States. In 1903 he joined the Fabian Society, with which he remained actively (though not always harmoniously) connected for a number of years. In 1909 he moved to London, and in 1912 bought a house at

Easton Park near Dunmow, Essex, which remained
his home until his wife's death in 1927.

The New Machiavelli (1911) marks a new departure
in Wells' creative work; the novel of ideas and of
problems in which the (fictional) story becomes
subordinate to the sociological and ideological
message. The works *Marriage* (1912), *The Passionate
Friends* (1913), *The Wife of Sir Isaac Harman* (1914),
The Research Magnificent (1915), belong to this
category.

Wells supported the first World War as the
" War to end War " and in 1918 became for a
short time director of Propaganda Policy against
Germany on Lord Northcliffe's Enemy Propaganda
Committee. His most important work, written and
published during the war was *Mr. Britling sees it
Through* (1916) which achieved tremendous
popularity.

Shortly after the war (1920) he visited Soviet
Russia and in 1921 he attended the Washington
Conference. In the years to follow he travelled
much, and spent many winters away from the
rigours of the English climate. Though he continued
writing novels—his most important novel of the
inter-war years was *The World of William Clissold*
(1926)—he concentrated more and more on the
propagating of ideas. The main thesis which he
expounded during the last two decades of his life
was that the human race must adapt itself to the
material forces it has created, or perish. The three
great works *Outline of History* (1920), *Science of Life*
(1929), and *The Work, Wealth and Happiness of Mankind* (1932), were all designed to popularise the
ideology appropriate to the task of creating a World

State—in his view the only alternative to a return to barbarism and to final annihilation. In 1934 he published two volumes of autobiography, *Experiment in Living*.

The second World War was to him the confirmation that mankind had indeed lost the mastery over the forces of its own making and was heading inexorably towards doom. His last work, *Mind at the End of its Tether* (1945), gave expression to his final mood of despair.

Having been ailing for some considerable time, he died in his London home on August 13th, 1946.

H. d. R.

INTRODUCTION

THE expressions "Scientific Romances" and
"Science Fiction" do not to-day conjure up
visions of the better type of story telling. Heroes
now are Supermen, they live on Superfoods, their
knowledge is Superscience, and they look like over-
stuffed pinheads. They never walk, they fly, and
their flight, probably carrying a motorcar, a bizarre
temple and a Supergirl under one arm, can easily
carry them from star to star. The scientific story
passed out of literature into strip pictures, and since
the disappearance of the silent film and with it the
ability to tell a story in pictures, has now developed
a strange literary form of its own where phrases,
sentences, lines and paragraphs have given way to
indescriminate balloons, containing spattered globs
of language that can, if it is worth doing at all,
be read in any order.

It must not be thought that this Superliterature
is limited in its scope and variety ; it is not all about
Supermen. Sometimes it is about Wondermen, who
live on Wonderfoods, who know Wonderscience, and
have sexless Wondergirls as their companions. At
the beginning of each story the Hero is just an
ordinary chap, easily identified as the reader
himself, who hears of a crisis and thereupon changes
in a single picture into a Superwonder: his chest
becomes enormous and his body covered with
beautiful muscles (we are reminded of that offer,

that we ignored, when we too could have had a
perfect body in forty days or money refunded), he
changes at the same time into bathing trunks, a
jersey with a common device upon it, and a cloak;
but his head, and presumably its contents, remains
unchanged in size. Physically he can now do anything; he flies through the air, lifts bridges and
buildings, darts restlessly from planet to planet,
looks through things and lives in a universe where
there are no natural laws except that everyone must
speak English and crime does not pay, even though
our hero is the only policeman. There are Wondermen, Marvels, Miraclemen, Supermen, Invincible-
men and men by many other names, but we cannot
in honesty say that they form the basis of any credit
to the art of story telling.

I do not think that H. G. Wells was a great
student of the Strip-comic genre, but in his own
observations on the art of the fantastic story he
makes it very clear why his succeed and these others
fail: " any one can invent human beings inside
out," and " nothing remains interesting where anything may happen." In each of H. G.'s stories there
is only one impossible hypothesis. He argues the
plausibility of that hypothesis in the language of the
scientist. In bygone days Magic was accepted and
a spell was sufficient to make invisibility plausible;
in these days there is no magic, but we are willing
to accept a phenomenon properly explained, whether
we understand the explanation or not. Having
made the one hypothesis, it is thrown into an
ordinary world; the marvel, the monster, the created
fantasy becomes as real and vivid as a dream and
inhabits the reader's own home.

In the latter half of the nineteenth century the scientific romance was more usually in the form of an imaginary journey. The majority of Jules Verne's novels take this form; the most successful of them were written in the ten years from 1862 to 1872. He takes his readers with great good nature for a five-week trip in a balloon, to the centre of the earth, ten thousand leagues under the sea, to the north pole and around the world. In 1895 H. G. Wells takes us for our first voyage with him, a journey in the Time Machine. In that same year Georges Méliès, a great pioneer of 'la Cinematographie' started his production of his fantastic films. Jules Verne took us *De la terre à la Lune* in 1865. H. G. Wells landed on the moon, with *The First Men in the Moon*, in 1901 and in the following year Georges Méliès gave us, in his three-hunredeth film, twelve minutes of a trip to the moon.

Jules Verne believed sincerely that the things he foretold would come about at some time in the future. He wrote saying, ' I tell you, this *will* happen! " H. G. Wells accepted, as many then did, that such things would one day be possible; he wrote saying, ' when it happens, this is how it will affect *you*.' Méliès, the conjuror-comedian, showed us in pictures how ridiculous it would be when we did such remarkable things.

This story of H. G.'s has itself been made as a film, memorable, if for nothing else, for the voice of Claude Rains, a man able and courageous enough to act without face or fingers and who, in his performance, touched the deep tragedy that the Invisible Man had to suffer.

To H. G. it was the effect that scientific progress

would have on the world, and the way in which
people would react to the coming wonders, that was
of the greatest importance. In *The Invisible Man* he
goes even deeper by studying the effect on the
individual. He restates the sad and relentless
cruelty of the mob to the unusual, to the hunchback,
the cross-eyed, the monster or the pathetic simpleton.
He lays before us the despair and loneliness of the
mob's victim, the schizm between the desperate
frightened individual out-of-joint and the close
unthinking mutually protective herd. Every action
on either side takes no count of the other: the
outcast is out and without thought or knowledge of
the crime there is no forgiveness from the rest.

This novel is more, then, than just a Scientific
Romance; it is the study of a character, a man who
strives to make himself unusual and thereby always
above his fellow men, a man that sees in himself and
his uniqueness a power over others, a man with the
very stuff that dictatorship is made of, the man
Griffin. He occurs in different forms in other H. G.
Wells novels: as Nunez who thinks to be King in
the Country of the Blind, and as Rudolph Whitlow
who is a Holy Terror from his birth to his death.
Griffin stumbles by an accident of his own intelligence upon the solution of that impossible hypothesis,
that a man can be invisible. Invisibility he achieves
without a Cloak, that magic cloak that gives its
wearer invisibility and, presumably, its wearer
obliges by making the cloak invisible too. Griffin
reaches the power, the dream of power that the
thought of invisibility conjures up in his mind, by
relentless labour; the invisibility that is his reward
is real, it does not touch his clothes, his undigested

meals, the mud that spatters him, or the silent snow that settles in his hair. He achieves the logically impossible and is left with a bitter reality, a power no greater than a help to petty larceny, a power more binding than chains, more empty than releasing death.

To Jules Verne Invisibility would have been an adventure into the unknown. To Méliès a slapstick frolic of trickery and illusion. Here, to H. G. Wells, it is a tragedy. The scientific worker strives continually to give man a greater power to shape his destiny; the individual finds more and more that he holds in his hands the power of life over death, and in its execution it operates only as a power of death over life. H. G. Wells foresaw the way the World is going and that the very knowledge that points that way, in the hands of single individuals, who being very ordinary and natural animals see themselves getting there first, can compass nothing but their own destruction. Such a one is Griffin, the Invisible Man. This book has in it a story to be cherished, not only for the understanding of the uniquitous and to-be-pitied ego-centric, but because it is of the golden age of the Scientific Romance.

In the fifty years after 1862, when Jules Verne was writing his first ' voyages imaginaires,' scientific nvention was profoundly affecting the way of life of ordinary people. In 1876 Thomas Edison made his first talking machines. In 1879, with J. W. Swan, he made the first practical electric light bulbs. In 1885 Daimler and Benz were working on the first internal combustion engined motorcars. In 1895 Marconi transmitted wireless messages, and in 1901 the first signals were sent and received across the

Atlantic Ocean. In 1903 the Wright brothers flew in the first successful heavier than air machine. Six years later Bleriot flew across the English Channel.

In those years people saw the coming of the horse-less carriage and in their life-times motorcars became commonplace. The instantaneous message became the everyday tool of the ordinary man. Light and Heat leapt to his fingertips. The normal things of middle-age had been childhood wonders.

In the days of Jules Verne and of the early novels of H. G. Wells scientific discovery and invention was dealing with things that could, like magic, be easily accepted. Their writings dealt with simple physical facts that the reader could grasp and did not have to understand: flying, journeying through space, travelling under the sea, making diamonds, travelling in time. Such things were daily coming true. It was an era of new horizons. The Inventor was concerned with making things go, where they did not go before.

Now, science is too difficult, too broad and too near. It appears that anything is possible so that there is no longer any adventure in simple things, nothing remains interesting where anything may happen. Science fiction can no longer discuss the plain effects of discovery on ordinary people; the ordinary people have experienced too much in their life-times. In 1900 the coming changes were exciting reading. Now we look only for the perfecting of the everyday things that we have already got; we expect to do things faster, more easily and a great deal more expensively tomorrow than we do them today. There are no new horizons—only extended horizons. It is stimulating to reach the top of a mountain and beyond the peak to see a new and unexplored country. But it is boring to climb up from ridge to ridge and never to reach the top, because the top is in infinity.

Yet in these novels of adventure into the unknown there are still some that have lost none of their magic. We shall reach the moon, we encircle the globe in a couple of days, we have been deep into the sea and the earth and we know that the North Pole is not there. But some things we shall never do although we can, in some accounts of them, believe in them. However cynical we become about ' science,' there are still mysteries, and we can read with the same feeling of reality, as we could have felt on the day when they were written, of working miracles, of travelling in time, and of the grotesque romance of *The Invisible Man.*

FRANK WELLS

CONTENTS

I

The Strange Man's Arrival

THE stranger came early in February, one wintry day, through a biting wind and a driving snow, the last snowfall of the year, over the down, walking from Bramblehurst Railway Station, and carrying a little black portmanteau in his thickly-gloved hand. He was wrapped up from head to foot, and the brim of his soft felt hat hid every inch of his face save the shiny tip of his nose; the snow had piled itself against his shoulders and chest, and added a white crest to the burden he carried. He staggered into the " Coach and Horses " more dead than alive, and flung his portmanteau down. " A fire," he cried, " in the name of human charity! A room and a fire! " He stamped and shook the snow from off himself in the bar, and followed Mrs. Hall into her guest parlour to strike his bargain. And with that much introduction, that and a couple of sovereigns flung upon the table, he took up his quarters in the inn.

Mrs. Hall lit the fire and left him there while she went to prepare him a meal with her own hands. A guest to stop at Iping in the winter time was an unheard-of piece of luck, let alone a guest who was no " haggler," and she was resolved to show herself worthy of her good fortune.

As soon as the bacon was well under way, and

Millie, her lymphatic aid, had been brisked up a bit by a few deftly chosen expressions of contempt, she carried the cloth, plates, and glasses into the parlour, and began to lay them with the utmost *éclat*. Although the fire was burning up briskly, she was surprised to see that her visitor still wore his hat and coat, and stood with his back to her and staring out of the window at the falling snow in the yard.

His gloved hands were clasped behind him, and he seemed to be lost in thought. She noticed that the melted snow that still sprinkled his shoulders dripped upon her carpet.

" Can I take your hat and coat, sir," she said, " and give them a good dry in the kitchen? "

" No," he said, without turning.

She was not sure she had heard him, and was about to repeat her question.

He turned his head and looked at her over his shoulder. " I prefer to keep them on," he said with emphasis; and she noticed that he wore big blue spectacles with side-lights, and had a bushy side whisker over his coat collar that completely hid his face.

" Very well, sir," she said. " *As* you like. In a bit the room will be warmer."

He made no answer, and turned his face away from her again, and Mrs. Hall, feeling that her conversational advances were ill-timed, laid the rest of the table things in a quick staccato manner, and whisked out of the room. When she returned he was still standing there like a man of stone, his back hunched, his collar turned up, his dripping hat-brim turned down, hiding his face and ears with

considerable emphasis, and called rather than said
to him:

"Your lunch is served, sir."

"Thank you," he said at the same time, and did
not stir until she was closing the door. Then he
swung round and approached the table with a
certain eagerness.

As she went behind the bar to the kitchen she
heard a sound repeated at regular intervals. Chirk,
chirk, chirk, it went, the sound of a spoon being
whisked rapidly round a basin. "That girl!" she
said. "There! I clean forgot it. It's her being so
long!" And while she herself finished mixing the
mustard, she gave Millie a few verbal stabs for her
excessive slowness. She had cooked the ham and
eggs, laid the table, and done everything, while
Millie (help, indeed!) had only succeeded in delaying
the mustard. And him a new guest, and wanting
to stay! Then she filled the mustard-pot, and,
putting it with some stateliness upon a gold and
black tea-tray, carried it into the parlour.

She rapped and entered promptly. As she did so
her visitor moved quickly, so that she got but a
glimpse of a white object disappearing behind the
table. It would seem he was picking something
from the floor. She rapped down the mustard-pot
on the table, and then she noticed the overcoat and
hat had been taken off and put over a chair in front
of the fire. A pair of wet boots threatened rust to
her steel fender.

She went to these things resolutely. "I suppose
I may have them to dry now?" she said, in a
voice that brooked no denial.

"Leave the hat," said her visitor in a muffled

voice, and turning, she saw he had raised his head and was looking at her.

For a moment she stood gazing at him, too surprised to speak.

He held a white cloth—it was a serviette he had brought with him—over the lower part of the face, so that his mouth and jaws were completely hidden, and that was the reason of his muffled voice. But it was not that which startled Mrs. Hall. It was the fact that all the forehead above his blue glasses was covered by a white bandage, and that another covered his ears, leaving not a scrap of his face exposed excepting only his pink, peaked nose. It was bright pink, and shining, just as it had been at first. He wore a dark brown velvet jacket, with a high, black, linen-lined collar turned up about his neck. The thick black hair, escaping as it could below and between the cross bandages, projected in curious tails and horns, giving him the strangest appearance conceivable. This muffled and bandaged head was so unlike what she had anticipated that for a moment she was rigid.

He did not remove the serviette, but remained holding it, as she saw now, with a brown gloved hand, and regarding her with his inscrutable blank glasses. "Leave the hat," he said, speaking indistinctly through the white cloth.

Her nerves began to recover from the shock they had received. She placed the hat on the chair again by the fire. "I didn't know, sir," she began, " that——" And she stopped, embarrassed.

"Thank you," he said dryly, glancing from her to the door, and then at her again.

"I'll have them nicely dried, sir, at once," she

said, and carried his clothes out of the room. She glanced at his white-swathed head and blank goggles again as she was going out of the door; but his napkin was still in front of his face. She shivered a little as she closed the door behind her, and her face was eloquent of her surprise and perplexity. " I *never*! " she whispered. " There! " She went quite softly to the kitchen, and was too preoccupied to ask Millie what she was messing about with *now*, when she got there.

The visitor sat and listened to her retreating feet. He glanced inquiringly at the window before he removed his serviette, and resumed his meal. He took a mouthful, glanced suspiciously at the window, took another mouthful; then rose and, taking the serviette in his hand, walked across the room and pulled the blind down to the top of the white muslin that obscured the lower panes. This plunged the room in twilight. He returned with an easier air to the table and his meal.

" The poor soul's had an accident, or an op'ration or somethin'," said Mrs. Hall. " What a turn them bandages did give me to be sure! "

She put on some more coal, unfolded the clothes-horse, and extended the traveller's coat upon this. " And the goggles! Why, he looked more like a divin' 'elmet than a human man! " She hung his muffler on a corner of the horse. " And holding that handkerchief over his mouth all the time. Talkin' through it! . . . Perhaps his mouth was hurt too—maybe."

She turned round, as one who suddenly remembers. " Bless my soul alive! " she said, going off at a tangent, " ain't you done them taters *yet*, Millie? "

When Mrs. Hall went to clear away the stranger's lunch her idea that his mouth must also have been cut or disfigured in the accident she supposed him to have suffered was confirmed, for he was smoking a pipe, and all the time that she was in the room he never loosened the silk muffler he had wrapped round the lower part of his face to put the mouth-piece to his lips. Yet it was not forgetfulness, for she saw he glanced at the tobacco as it smouldered out. He sat in the corner with his back to the window-blind, and spoke now, having eaten and drunk and being comfortably warmed through, with less aggressive brevity than before. The reflection of the fire lent a kind of red animation to his big spectacles they had lacked hitherto.

" I have some luggage," he said, " at Bramble-hurst Station," and he asked her how he could have it sent. He bowed his bandaged head quite politely in acknowledgment of her explanation.   " To-morrow! " he said. " There is no speedier delivery?" and seemed disappointed when she answered " No." " Was she quite sure? No man with a trap who would go over? "

Mrs. Hall, nothing loath, answered his questions, and then developed a conversation. " It's a steep road by the down, sir," she said, in answer to the question about a trap; and then snatching at an opening said " It was there a carriage was upsettled, a year ago and more. A gentleman killed, besides his coachman. Accidents, sir, happen in a moment, don't they? "

But the visitor was not to be drawn so easily. " They do," he said, through his muffler, eyeing her quietly from behind his impenetrable glasses.

"But they take long enough to get well, sir, don't they? There was my sister's son, Tom, jest cut his arm with a scythe—tumbled on it in the 'ayfield— and bless me! he was three months tied up, sir. You'd hardly believe it. It's regular give me a dread of a scythe, sir."

"I can quite understand that," said the visitor.

"We was afraid, one time, that he'd have to have an op'ration, he was that bad, sir."

The visitor laughed abruptly—a bark of a laugh that he seemed to bite and kill in his mouth. "*Was* he?" he said.

"He was, sir. And no laughing matter to them as had the doing for him as I had, my sister being took up with her little ones so much. There was bandages to do, sir, and bandages to undo. So that if I may make so bold as to say it, sir——"

"Will you get me some matches?" said the visitor quite abruptly. "My pipe is out."

Mrs. Hall was pulled up suddenly. It was certainly rude of him after telling him all she had done. She gasped at him for a moment, and remembered the two sovereigns. She went for the matches.

"Thanks," he said concisely, as she put them down, and turned his shoulder upon her and stared out of the window again. Evidently he was sensitive on the topic of operations and bandages. She did not "make so bold as to say," after all. But his snubbing way had irritated her, and Millie had a hot time of it that afternoon.

The visitor remained in the parlour until four o'clock, without giving the ghost of an excuse for an intrusion. For the most part he was quite still during that time; it would seem he sat in the growing darkness, smoking by the firelight—perhaps dozing.

Once or twice a curious listener might have heard him at the coals, and for the space of five minutes he was audible pacing the room. He seemed to be talking to himself. Then the arm-chair creaked as he sat down again.

2

Mr. Teddy Henfrey's First Impressions

AT four o'clock, when it was fairly dark, and Mrs. Hall was screwing up her courage to go in and ask her visitor if he would take some tea, Teddy Henfrey, the clock-jobber, came into the bar.

"My sakes, Mrs. Hall," said he, "but this is terrible weather for thin boots!" The snow outside was falling faster.

Mrs. Hall agreed, and then noticed he had his bag with him. "Now you're here, Mr. Teddy," said she, "I'd be glad if you'd give th' old clock in the parlour a bit of a look. 'Tis going, and it strikes well, and hearty, but the hour hand won't do nuthin' but point at six."

And leading the way, she went across to the parlour door and rapped and entered.

Her visitor, she saw, as she opened the door, was seated in the arm-chair before the fire, dozing, it would seem, with his bandaged head drooping on one side. The only light in the room was the red glow from the fire. Everything was ruddy, shadowy, and indistinct to her, the more so since she had just been lighting the bar lamp, and her eyes were dazzled. But for a second it seemed to her that the man she looked at had an enormous mouth wide open, a vast and incredible mouth that swallowed the whole of the lower portion of his face. It was the sensation of a moment; the white-bound head, the monstrous goggle eyes, and this huge yawn below it. Then he stirred, started up in his chair, put up his hand. She opened the door wide so that the room was lighter, and she saw him more clearly, with the muffler held to his face, just as she had seen him hold the serviette before. The shadows, she fancied, had tricked her.

"Would you mind, sir, this man a-coming to look at the clock, sir?" she said, recovering from her momentary disorder.

"Look at the clock?" he said, staring round in a drowsy manner, and speaking over his hand; and then, getting more fully awake, "Certainly."

Mrs. Hall went away to get a lamp, and he rose and stretched himself. Then came the light, and Mr. Teddy Henfrey, entering, was confronted by this bandaged person. He was, he says, "taken aback."

"Good afternoon," said the stranger, regarding him—as Mr. Henfrey says, with a vivid sense of the dark spectacles—"like a lobster."

"I hope," said Mr. Henfrey, "that it's no intrusion."

"None whatever," said the stranger. "Though I understand," he said, turning to Mrs. Hall, "that this room is really to be mine for my own private use."

"I thought, sir," said Mrs. Hall, "you'd prefer the clock——"

"Certainly," said the stranger, "certainly; but as a rule I like to be alone and undisturbed."

He turned round with his back to the fireplace, and put his hands behind his back. "And presently," he said, "when the clock-mending is over,

I think I should like to have some tea. But not till
the clock-mending is over."

Mrs. Hall was about to leave the room—she made
no conversational advances this time, because she
did not want to be snubbed in front of Mr. Henfrey
—when her visitor asked her if she had made any
arrangements about his boxes at Bramblehurst. She
told him she had mentioned the matter to the postman, and that the carrier could bring them over
on the morrow.

" You are certain that is the earliest? " he said.

She was certain, with a marked coolness.

" I should explain," he added, " what I was really
too cold and fatigued to do before, that I am an
experimental investigator."

" Indeed, sir," said Mrs. Hall, much impressed.

" And my baggage contains apparatus and
appliances."

" Very useful things indeed they are, sir," said
Mrs. Hall.

" And I'm naturally anxious to get on with my
inquiries."

" Of course, sir."

" My reason for coming to Iping," he proceeded,
with a certain deliberation of manner, " was . . .
a desire for solitude. I do not wish to be disturbed in my work. In addition to my work, an
accident——"

" I thought as much," said Mrs. Hall to herself.

" Necessitates a certain retirement. My eyes are
sometimes so weak and painful that I have to shut
myself up in the dark for hours together—lock
myself up. Sometimes—now and then. Not at
present, certainly. At such times the slightest disturb-

ance, the entry of a stranger into the room, is a source of excruciating annoyance to me. . . . It is well these things should be understood."

"Certainly, sir," said Mrs. Hall. "And if I might make so bold as to ask——"

"That, I think, is all," said the stranger, with that quietly irresistible air of finality he could assume at will. Mrs. Hall reserved her question and sympathy for a better occasion.

After Mrs. Hall had left the room he remained standing in front of the fire, glaring, so Mr. Henfrey puts it, at the clock-mending. Mr. Henfrey worked with the lamp close to him, and the green shade threw a brilliant light upon his hands and upon the frame and wheels, and left the rest of the room shadowy. When he looked up coloured patches swam in his eyes. Being constitutionally of a curious nature, he had removed the works—a quite unnecessary proceeding—with the idea of delaying his departure and perhaps falling into conversation with the stranger. But the stranger stood there, perfectly silent and still. So still—it got on Henfrey's nerves. He felt alone in the room and looked up, and there, grey and dim, was the bandaged head and huge, dark lenses, staring fixedly, with a mist of green spots drifting in front of them. It was so uncanny to Henfrey that for a minute they remained staring blankly at one another. Then Henfrey looked down again. Very uncomfortable position! One would like to say something. Should he remark that the weather was very cold for the time of the year?

He looked up as if to take aim with that introductory shot. "The weather——" he began.

"Why don't you finish and go?" said the rigid figure, evidently in a state of painfully suppressed rage. "All you've got to do is to fix the hour hand on its—axle. You're simply humbugging."

"Certainly, sir—one minute more. I overlooked . . ." And Mr. Henfrey finished and went.

But he went off feeling excessively annoyed. "Damn it!" said Mr. Henfrey to himself, trudging down the village through the falling snow, "a man must do a clock at times, sure-*ly*."

And again, "Can't a man look at you? Ugly!"

And yet again, "Seemingly not. If the police was wanting you, you couldn't be more wrapped and bandaged."

At Gleeson's corner he saw Hall, who had recently married the stranger's hostess at the "Coach and Horses," and who now drove the Iping conveyance, when occasional people required it, to Sidderbridge Junction, coming towards him on his return from that place. Hall had evidently been "stopping a bit" at Sidderbridge, to judge by his driving. "'Ow do, Teddy?" he said, passing.

"You got a rum un up home!" said Teddy.

Hall very sociably pulled up. "What's that?" he asked.

"Rum-looking customer stopping at the 'Coach and Horses,'" said Teddy. "My sakes!"

And he proceeded to give Hall a vivid description of his wife's grotesque guest. "Looks a bit like a disguise, don't it? I'd like to see a man's face if I had him stopping in *my* place," said Henfrey. "But women are that trustful—where strangers are concerned. He's took your rooms, and he ain't even given a name, Hall."

"You don't say so," said Hall, who was a man of sluggish apprehension.

"Yes," said Teddy. "By the week. Whatever he is, you can't get rid of him under the week. And he's got a lot of luggage coming to-morrow, so he says. Let's hope it won't be stones in boxes, Hall."

He told Hall how his aunt at Hastings had been swindled by a stranger with empty portmanteaux. Altogether he left Hall vaguely suspicious. "Get up, old girl," said Hall. "I 'spose I must see 'bout this."

Teddy trudged on his way with his mind considerably relieved.

Instead of "seeing 'bout it," however, Hall, on his return, was severely rated by his wife on the length of time he had spent in Sidderbridge, and his mild inquiries were answered snappishly and in a manner not to the point. But the seed of suspicion Teddy had sown germinated in the mind of Mr. Hall in spite of these discouragements. "You wim' don't know everything," said Mr. Hall, resolved to ascertain more about the personality of his guest at the earliest possible opportunity. And after the stranger had gone to bed, which he did about half-past nine, Mr. Hall went aggressively into the parlour, and looked very hard at his wife's furniture, just to show that the stranger wasn't master there, and scrutinised a little contemptuously a sheet of mathematical computations the stranger had left. When retiring for the night, he instructed Mrs. Hall to look very closely at the stranger's luggage when it came next day.

"You mind your own business, Hall," said Mrs. Hall, "and I'll mind mine."

She was all the more inclined to snap at Hall because the stranger was undoubtedly an unusually strange sort of stranger, and she was by no means assured about him in her own mind. In the middle of the night she woke up dreaming of huge, white heads like turnips, that came trailing after her, at the end of interminable necks, and with vast black eyes. But being a sensible woman, she subdued her terrors, and turned over and went to sleep again.

3

The Thousand and One Bottles

So it was that on the 9th day of February, at the beginning of the thaw, this singular person fell out of infinity into Iping village. Next day his luggage arrived through the slush—and very remarkable luggage it was. There were a couple of trunks, indeed, such as a rational man might have, but in addition there were a box of books—big, fat books, of which some were just in an incomprehensible handwriting—and a dozen or more crates, boxes, and cases, containing objects packed in straw—glass bottles, as it seemed to Hall, tugging with a casual curiosity at the straw. The stranger, muffled in hat, coat, gloves, and wrapper, came out impatiently to meet Fearenside's cart, while Hall was having a word or so of gossip preparatory to helping bring them in. Out he came, not noticing Fearenside's dog, who was sniffing in a *dilettante* spirit at Hall's legs.

" Come along with those boxes," he said. " I've been waiting long enough."

And he came down the steps towards the tail of the wagon, as if to lay hands on the smaller crate.

No sooner had Fearenside's dog caught sight of him, however, than it began to bristle and growl savagely, and when he rushed down the steps it gave an undecided hop, and then sprang straight at his hand. " Whup! " cried Hall, jumping back, for he was no hero with dogs, and Fearenside howled, " Lie down! " and snatched his whip.

They saw the dog's teeth had slipped the hand, heard a kick, saw the dog execute a flanking jump and get home on the stranger's leg, and heard the rip of his trousering. Then the finer end of Fearenside's whip reached his property, and the dog, yelping with dismay, retreated under the wheels of the wagon. It was all the business of a swift half minute. No one spoke, everyone shouted. The stranger glanced swiftly at his torn glove and at his leg, made as if he would stoop to the latter, then turned and rushed up the steps into the inn. They heard him go headlong across the passage and up the uncarpeted stairs to his bedroom.

" You brute, you! " said Fearenside, climbing off the wagon with his whip in his hand, while the dog watched him through the wheel.

" Come here! " said Fearenside. . . . " You'd better."

Hall had stood gaping. " He wuz bit," said Hall. " I'd better go an' see to en." And he trotted after the stranger. He met Mrs. Hall in the passage. " Carrier's darg," he said, " bit en."

He went straight upstairs, and the stranger's door being ajar, he pushed it open, and was entering without any ceremony, being of a naturally sympathetic turn of mind.

The blind was down and the room dim. He caught a glimpse of a most singular thing, what seemed a handless arm waving towards him, and a face of three huge, indeterminate spots on white, very like the face of a pale pansy. Then he was struck violently in the chest, hurled back, and the door slammed in his face, and locked. It was so rapid that it gave him no time to observe. A waving of indecipherable shapes, a blow and a concussion. There he stood on the dark little landing, wondering what it might be that he had seen.

After a couple of minutes he rejoined the little group that had formed outside the " Coach and Horses." There was Fearenside telling about it all over again for the second time; there was Mrs. Hall saying his dog didn't have no business to bite her guests; there was Huxter, the general dealer from over the road, interrogative: and Sandy Wadgers from the forge, judicial; besides women and children, all of them saying fatuities: " Wouldn't let en bite *me*, I knows "; " 'Tasn't right *have* such dargs "; " What '*e* bite 'n for; then? " and so forth.

Mr. Hall, staring at them from the steps and listening, found it incredible that he had seen anything so very remarkable happen upstairs. Besides, his vocabulary was altogether too limited for his impressions.

" He don't want no help, he says," he said in answer to his wife's inquiry. " We'd better be a-takin' of his luggage in."

" He ought to have it cauterised at once," said Mr. Huxter, " especially if it's at all inflamed."

" I'd shoot en, that's what I'd do," said a lady in the group.

Suddenly the dog began growling again.

" Come along," cried an angry voice in the doorway, and there stood the muffled stranger, with his collar turned up and his hat brim bent down. " The sooner you get those things in the better I'll be pleased." It is stated by an anonymous bystander that his trousers and gloves had been changed.

"Was you hurt, sir?" said Fearenside. "I'm rare sorry the darg——"

"Not a bit," said the stranger. "Never broke the skin. Hurry up with those things."

He then swore to himself, so Mr. Hall asserts.

Directly the first crate was, in accordance with his directions, carried into the parlour, the stranger flung himself upon it with extraordinary eagerness and began to unpack it, scattering the straw with an utter disregard of Mrs. Hall's carpet, and from it he began to produce bottles—little fat bottles containing powders, small and slender bottles containing coloured and white fluids, fluted blue bottles labelled *poison*, bottles with round bodies and slender necks, large green glass bottles, large white glass bottles, bottles with glass stoppers and frosted labels, bottles with fine corks, bottles with bungs, bottles with wooden caps, wine bottles, salad-oil bottles— putting them in rows on the chiffonier, on the mantle, on the table under the window, round the floor, on the book-shelf—everywhere. The chemist's shop in Bramblehurst could not boast half so many. Quite a sight it was. Crate after crate yielded bottles, until all six were empty and the table high with straw; the only things that came out of these crates besides the bottles were a number of test tubes and a carefully packed balance.

And directly the crates were unpacked the stranger went to the window and set to work, not troubling in the least about the litter of straw, the fire which had gone out, the box of books outside, nor for the trunks and other luggage that had gone upstairs.

When Mrs. Hall took his dinner in to him, he was already so absorbed in his work, pouring little drops out of the bottles into test tubes, that he did not hear her until she had swept away the bulk of the straw and put the tray on the table, with some little emphasis perhaps, seeing the state that the floor was in. Then he half turned his head, and immediately turned it away again. But she saw he had removed his glasses; they were beside him on the table, and it seemed to her that his eye sockets were extraordinarily hollow. He put on his spectacles again, and then turned and faced her. She was about to complain of the straw on the floor when he anticipated her.

" I wish you wouldn't come in without knocking," he said, in the tone of abnormal exasperation that seemed so characteristic of him.

" I knocked, but seemingly——"

" Perhaps you did. But in my investigations—my really very urgent and necessary investigations—the slightest disturbance, the jar of a door. . . . I must ask you——"

" Certainly, sir. You can turn the lock if you're like that, you know. Any time."

" A very good idea," said the stranger.

" This stror, sir. If I might make so bold as to remark——"

" Don't. If the straw makes trouble, put it down in the bill." And he mumbled at her—words suspiciously like curses.

He was so odd, standing there, so aggressive and explosive, bottle in one hand and test tube in the other, that Mrs. Hall was quite alarmed. But she was a resolute woman. " In which case, I should like to know, sir, what you consider——"

" A shilling—put down a shilling. Surely a shilling's enough? "

" So be it," said Mrs. Hall, taking up the table-cloth and beginning to spread it over the table. " If you're satisfied, of course——"

He turned and sat down with his coat collar towards her.

All the afternoon he worked with the door locked, and, as Mrs. Hall testifies, for the most part in silence. But once there was a concussion and a sound of bottles ringing together, as though the table had been hit, and the smash of glass flung violently down, and then a rapid pacing athwart the room. Fearing something was the matter, she went to the door and listened, not caring to knock.

" I can't go on," he was raving; " I *can't* go on! Three hundred thousand, four hundred thousand! The huge multitude! Cheated! All my life it may take me! . . . Patience! Patience, indeed! . . . Fool! fool! "

There was a noise of hobnails on the bricks in the bar, and Mrs. Hall very reluctantly had to leave the rest of his soliloquy. When she returned the room was silent again, save for the faint crepitation of his chair and the occasional clink of a bottle. It was all over; the stranger had resumed work.

When she took in his tea she saw broken glass in the corner of the room under the concave mirror, and a golden stain that had been carelessly wiped. She called attention to it.

" Put it down in the bill," snapped her visitor.

" For God's sake don't worry me! If there's damage done, put it down in the bill," and he went on ticking a list in the exercise-book before him.

. . . . . .

" I'll tell you something," said Fearenside mysteriously. It was late in the afternoon and they were in the little beershop of Iping Hanger.

" Well? " said Teddy Henfrey.

" This chap you're speaking of, what my darg bit. Well—he's black. Leastways his legs are.

" I seed through the tear of his trousers and the tear of his glove. You'd have expected a sort of pinky to show, wouldn't you? Well—there wasn't none. Just blackness. I tell you he's as black as my hat."

" My sakes! " said Henfrey. " It's a rummy case altogether. Why, his nose is as pink as paint! "

" That's true," said Fearenside. " I knows that. And I tell 'ee what I'm thinking. That marn's a piebald, Teddy; black here and white there—in patches. And he's ashamed of it. He's a kind of half-breed, and the colour's come off patchy instead of mixing. I've heard of such things before. And it's the common way with harrses, as anyone can see."

4

Mr. Cuss Interviews the Stranger

I HAVE told the circumstances of the stranger's arrival in Iping with a certain fullness of detail, in order that the curious impression he created may be understood by the reader. But excepting two odd incidents, the circumstances of his stay until the extraordinary day of the club festival may be passed over very cursorily. There were a number of skirmishes with Mrs. Hall in matters of domestic discipline, but in every case until late in April, when the first signs of penury began, he overrode her by the easy expedient of an extra payment. Hall did not like him, and whenever he dared he talked of the advisability of getting rid of him; but he showed his dislike mainly by concealing it ostentatiously, and avoiding his visitor as much as possible. "Wait till the summer," said Mrs. Hall sagely, "when the artisks are beginning to come. Then we'll see. He may be a bit overbearing, but bills settled punctual is bills settled punctual, whatever you likes to say."

The stranger did not go to church, and indeed made no difference between Sunday and the irreligious days, even in costume. He worked, as Mrs. Hall thought, very fitfully. Some days he would come down early and be continuously busy. On others he would rise late, pace his room, fretting audibly for hours together, smoke, or sleep in the arm-chair by the fire. Communication with the world beyond the village he had none. His temper continued very uncertain; for the most part his manner was that of a man suffering under almost unendurable provocation, and once or twice things were snapped, torn, crushed, or broken in spasmodic gusts of violence. His habit of talking to himself in a low voice grew steadily upon him, but though Mrs. Hall listened conscientiously she could make neither head nor tail of what she heard.

He rarely went abroad by day, but at twilight he would go out muffled up enormously, whether the weather was cold or not, and he chose the loneliest paths and those most over-shadowed by trees and banks. His goggling spectacles and ghastly, bandaged face under the penthouse of his hat, came with a disagreeable suddenness out of the darkness upon one or two home-going labourers; and Teddy Henfrey, tumbling out of the " Scarlet Coat " one night at half-past nine, was scared shamefully by the stranger's skull-like head (he was walking hat in hand) lit by the sudden light of the opened inn door. Such children as saw him at nightfall dreamt of bogies, and it seemed doubtful whether he disliked boys more than they disliked him, or the reverse; but there was certainly a vivid enough dislike on either side.

It was inevitable that a person of so remarkable an appearance and bearing should form a frequent topic in such a village as Iping. Opinion was greatly divided about his occupation. Mrs. Hall was sensitive on the point. When questioned, she explained very carefully that he was an " experimental investigator," going gingerly over the syllables as one who dreads pitfalls. When asked what an experimental investigator was, she would say with a touch of superiority that most educated people knew such things as that, and would then explain that he " discovered things." Her visitor had had an accident, she said, which temporarily discoloured his face and hands, and being of a sensitive disposition was averse to any public notice of the fact.

Out of her hearing there was a view largely entertained that he was a criminal trying to escape from justice by wrapping himself altogether from the eye of the police. This idea sprang from the brain of Mr. Teddy Henfrey. No crime of any magnitude dating from the middle or end of February was known to have occurred. Elaborated in the imagination of Mr. Gould, the probationary assistant in the National School, this theory took the form that the stranger was an anarchist in disguise, preparing explosives, and he resolved to undertake such detective operations as his time permitted. These consisted for the most part in looking very hard at the stranger whenever they met, or in asking people who had never seen the stranger leading questions about him. But he detected nothing.

Another school of opinion followed Mr. Fearenside, and either accepted the piebald view or some modification of it. As, for instance, Silas Durgan who was heard to assert that " if he chose to show enself at fairs he'd make his fortune in no time," and being a bit of a theologian compared the stranger to the man with the one talent. Yet another view explained the entire matter by regarding the stranger as a harmless lunatic. That had the advantage of accounting for everything straight away. Between these main groups there were waverers and compromisers. Sussex folk have few superstitions, and it was only after the events of early April that the thought of the supernatural was first whispered in the village. Even then it was only credited among the women folk.

But whenever they thought of him, people in Iping on the whole agreed in disliking him. His irritability, though it might have been comprehensible to an urban brain-worker, was an amazing thing to these quiet Sussex villagers. The frantic gesticulations they surprised now and then, the headlong pace after nightfall that swept him upon them round quiet corners, the inhuman bludgeoning of all the tentative advances of curiosity, the taste for twilight that led to the closing of doors, the pulling down of blinds, the extinction of candles and lamps—who could agree with such goings on? They drew aside as he passed down the village, and when he had gone by, young humorists would up with coat collars and down with hat brims, and go pacing nervously after him in imitation of his occult bearing. There was a song popular at that time called " The Bogey Man! " Miss Satchell sang it at the schoolroom concert—in aid of the church lamps—and thereafter, whenever one or two of the villagers were gathered together and the stranger appeared, a bar or so of this tune, more or less sharp or flat, was whistled in the midst of them. Also belated little children would call " Bogey Man! " after him, and make off, tremulously elated.

Cuss, the general practitioner, was devoured by

curiosity. The bandages excited his professional interest; the report of the thousand-and-one bottles aroused his jealous regard. All through April and May he coveted an opportunity of talking to the stranger, and at last, towards Whitsuntide, he could stand it no longer, but hit upon the subscription list for a village nurse as an excuse. He was surprised to find that Mrs. Hall did not know her guest's name.

" He gave a name," said Mrs. Hall—an assertion which was quite unfounded—" but I didn't rightly hear it." She thought it seemed so silly not to know the man's name.

Cuss rapped at the parlour door and entered. There was a fairly audible imprecation from within.

" Pardon my intrusion," said Cuss, and then the door closed and cut Mrs. Hall off from the rest of the conversation.

She could hear the murmur of voices for the next ten minutes, then a cry of surprise, a stirring of feet, a chair flung aside, a bark of laughter, quick steps to the door, and Cuss appeared, his face white, his eyes staring over his shoulder. He left the door open behind him, and, without looking at her, strode across the hall and went down the steps, and she heard his feet hurrying along the road. He carried his hat in his hand. She stood behind the bar, looking at the open door of the parlour. Then she heard the stranger laughing quietly, and his footsteps came across the room. She could not see his face where she stood. The parlour door slammed, and the place was silent again.

Cuss went straight up the village to Bunting, the vicar.

"Am I mad?" Cuss began abruptly, as he entered the shabby little study. "Do I look like an insane person?"

"What's happened?" said the vicar, putting the ammonite on the loose sheets of his forthcoming sermon.

"That chap at the inn——"

"Well?"

"Give me something to drink," said Cuss, and he sat down.

When his nerves had been steadied by a glass of cheap sherry—the only drink the good vicar had available—he told him of the interview he had just had.

"Went in," he gasped, "and began to demand a subscription for that nurse fund. He'd stuck his hands in his pockets as I came in, and he sat down lumpily in his chair. Sniffed. I told him I'd heard he took an interest in scientific things. He said, 'Yes.' Sniffed again. Kept on sniffing all the time, evidently recently caught an infernal cold. No wonder—wrapped up like that. I developed the nurse idea, and all the while kept my eyes open. Bottles—chemicals—everywhere. Balance, test tubes, in stands, and a smell of—evening primrose. Would he subscribe? Said he'd consider it. Asked him point blank was he researching. Said he was. A long research? Got quite cross, a 'damnable long research,' said he, blowing the cork out, so to speak. 'Oh?' said I. And out came the grievance. The man was just on the boil, and my question boiled him over. He had been given a prescription—most valuable prescription—what for he wouldn't say. Was it medical? 'Damn you! what are you fishing after?' I apologised. Dignified sniff and cough. He resumed. He'd read it. Five ingredients. Put it down; turned his head. Draught of air from window lifted the paper. Swish, rustle. He was working in a room with an open fireplace, he said. Saw a flicker, and there was the prescription burning and lifting chimneyward. Rushed towards it just as it whisked up chimney. So! Just at that point, to illustrate his story, out came his arm."

" Well? "

" No hand. Just an empty sleeve. Lord! I thought, *that's* a deformity! Got a cork arm, I suppose, and has taken it off. Then, I thought, there's something odd in that. What the devil keeps that sleeve up and open if there's nothing in it? There was nothing in it, I tell you. Nothing down it, right down to the joint. I could see right down it to the elbow, and there was a glimmer of light shining through a tear of the cloth. ' Good God! ' I said. Then he stopped. Stared at me with those blank, goggled eyes of his, and then at his sleeve."

" Well? "

" That's all. He never said a word, just glared and put his sleeve back in his pocket quickly. ' I was saying,' said he, ' that there was the prescription burning, wasn't I? ' Interrogative cough. ' How the devil,' said I, ' can you move an empty sleeve like that? ' ' Empty sleeve? ' ' Yes,' said I, ' an empty sleeve.'

" ' It's an empty sleeve, is it? You saw it was an empty sleeve? ' He stood up right away. I stood up too. He came towards me in three very slow steps, and stood quite close. Sniffed venomously.

I didn't flinch, though I'm hanged if that bandaged knob of his, and those blinkers, aren't enough to unnerve any one, coming quietly up to you.'

" ' You said it was an empty sleeve? ' he said. ' Certainly,' I said. At staring and saying nothing a bare-faced man, unspectacled, starts scratch. Then very quietly he pulled his sleeve out of his pocket again, and raised his arm towards me, as though he would show it to me again. He did it very, very slowly. I looked at it. Seemed an age. ' Well? ' said I, clearing my throat; ' there's nothing in it.'

" Had to say something. I was beginning to feel frightened. I could see right down it. He extended it straight towards me, slowly, slowly—just like that —until the cuff was six inches from my face. Queer thing to see an empty sleeve come at you like that! And then——"

" Well? "

" Something—exactly like a finger and a thumb it felt—nipped my nose."

Bunting began to laugh.

" There wasn't anything there! " said Cuss—his voice running up into a shriek at the " there." " It's all very well for you to laugh, but I tell you I was so startled, I hit his cuff hard, and turned round and cut out of the room—I left him——"

Cuss stopped. There was no mistaking the sincerity of his panic. He turned round in a helpless way, and took a second glass of the excellent vicar's very inferior sherry. " When I hit his cuff," said Cuss, " I tell you, it felt exactly like hitting an arm.

"And there wasn't an arm! There wasn't the ghost of an arm!"

Mr. Bunting thought it over. He looked suspiciously at Cuss. "It's a most remarkable story," he said. He looked very wise and grave indeed. "It's really," said Mr. Bunting with judicial emphasis, "a most remarkable story."

5

The Burglary at the Vicarage

THE facts of the burglary at the Vicarage come to us chiefly through the medium of the vicar and his wife. It occurred in the small hours of Whit Monday, the day devoted in Iping to the Club festivities. Mrs. Bunting, it seems, woke up suddenly in the stillness that comes before the dawn, with a strong impression that the door of their bedroom had opened and closed. She did not arouse her husband at first, but sat up in bed listening. She then distinctly heard the pad, pad, pad of bare feet coming out of the adjoining dressing-room and walking along the passage towards the staircase. So soon as she felt assured of this, she aroused the Rev. Mr. Bunting as quietly as possible. He did not strike a light, but putting on his spectacles, his dressing gown, and his bath slippers, went out on the landing to listen. He heard quite distinctly a fumbling going on at his study desk downstairs, and then a violent sneeze.

At that he returned to his bedroom, armed himself with the most obvious weapon, the poker, and descended the staircase as noiselessly as possible. Mrs. Bunting came out on the landing.

The hour was about four, and the ultimate darkness of the night was passed. There was a faint shimmer of light in the hall, but the study doorway yawned impenetrably black. Everything was still, except the faint creaking of the stairs under Mr. Bunting's tread, and the slight movements in the study. Then something snapped, the drawer was opened, and there was a rustle of papers. Then came an imprecation, and a match was struck, and the study was flooded with yellow light. Mr. Bunting was now in the hall, and through the crack of the door he could see the desk and the open drawer, and a candle burning on the desk. But the robber he could not see. He stood there in the hall undecided what to do, and Mrs. Bunting, her face white and intent, crept slowly downstairs after him. One thing kept up Mr. Bunting's courage. The persuasion that this burglar was a resident in the village.

They heard the chink of money, and realised that the robber had found the housekeeping reserve of gold—two pounds ten in half sovereigns altogether. At that sound Mr. Bunting was nerved to abrupt action. Gripping the poker firmly, he rushed into the room, closely followed by Mrs. Bunting.

" Surrender! " cried Mr. Bunting fiercely, and then stopped, amazed. Apparently the room was perfectly empty.

Yet their conviction that they had that very moment heard somebody moving in the room had amounted to a certainty. For half a minute perhaps they stood gasping, then Mrs. Bunting went across the room and looked behind the screen, while Mr. Bunting, by a kindred impulse, peered under the desk. Then Mrs. Bunting turned back the window curtains and Mr. Bunting looked up the chimney, and probed it with the poker. Then Mrs. Bunting

scrutinised the waste-paper basket, and Mr. Bunting
opened the coal-scuttle. Then they came to a stop,
and stood with eyes interrogating one another.

" I could have sworn——" said Mr. Bunting.

" The candle! " said Mr. Bunting. " Who lit the
candle? "

" The drawer! " said Mrs. Bunting. " And the
money's gone! "

She went hastily to the doorway.

" Of all the extraordinary occurrences——"

There was a violent sneeze in the passage. They
rushed out, and as they did so the kitchen door
slammed.

" Bring the candle! " said Mr. Bunting, and led
the way. They both heard the sound of bolts
being hastily shot back.

As he opened the kitchen door he saw through
the scullery that the back door was just opening,
and the faint light of early dawn displayed the dark
masses of the garden beyond. He was certain that
nothing went out of the door. It opened, stood open
for a moment, and then closed with a slam. As it
did so, the candle Mrs. Bunting was bringing from
the study flickered and flared. . . . It was a minute
or more before they entered the kitchen.

The place was empty. They refastened the back
door, examined the kitchen, pantry, and scullery
thoroughly, and at last went down into the cellar.
There was not a soul to be found in the house,
search as they would.

Daylight found the vicar and his wife, a quaintly
costumed little couple, still marvelling about on
their own ground floor by the unnecessary light of
a guttering candle.

"Of all the extraordinary affairs," began the vicar for the twentieth time.

"My dear," said Mrs. Bunting, "there's Susie coming down. Just wait here until she has gone into the kitchen, and then slip upstairs."

6

The Furniture that Went Mad

Now it happened that in the early hours of Whit Monday, before Millie was hunted out for the day, Mr. Hall and Mrs. Hall both rose and went noiselessly down into the cellar. Their business there was of a private nature, and had something to do with the specific gravity of their beer.

They had hardly entered the cellar when Mrs. Hall found she had forgotten to bring down a bottle of sarsaparilla from their joint room. As she was the expert and principal operator in this affair, Hall very properly went upstairs for it.

On the landing he was surprised to see that the stranger's door was ajar. He went on into his own room and found the bottle as he had been directed.

But as he came downstairs, he noticed that the bolts on the front door had been shot back—that the door was, in fact, simply on the latch. And, with a flash of inspiration, he connected this with the stranger's room upstairs and the suggestions of Mr. Teddy Henfrey. He distinctly remembered holding the candle while Mrs. Hall shot these bolts overnight. At the sight he stopped, gaping; then, with the bottle still in his hands, went upstairs again. He rapped at the stranger's door. There was no answer. He rapped again; then pushed the door wide open and entered.

It was as he expected. The bed, the room also, was empty. And what was queerer, even to his heavy intelligence, on the bedroom chair and along the rail of the bed were scattered the garments, the only garments so far as he knew, and the bandages of their guest. His big slouch hat even was cocked jauntily over the bedpost.

As Hall stood there he heard his wife's voice coming out of the depth of the cellar, and with that rapid telescoping of the syllables and interrogative cocking up of the final words to a high note, by which the West Sussex villager is wont to indicate a brisk impatience. " Gearge! You gart whad a wand? "

At that he turned and hurried down to her.

" Janny," he said over the rail of the cellar steps, " 'tas the truth what Henfrey sez. 'E's not in uz room, 'e en't. And the front door's onbolted."

At first Mrs. Hall did not understand, and so soon as she did she resolved to see the empty room for herself. Hall, still holding the bottle, went first. " If 'e en't there," he said, " 'is close are. And what's 'e doin' 'ithout 'is close, than? 'Tas a most curius basness."

As they came up the cellar steps they both, it was afterwards ascertained, fancied they heard the front door open and shut, but, seeing it closed and nothing there, neither said a word to the other about it at the time. Mrs. Hall passed her husband in the passage, and ran on first upstairs. Someone sneezed on the staircase. Hall, following six steps behind, thought that he heard her sneeze; she, going on first, was under the impression that Hall was sneezing. She flung open the door and

stood regarding the room. " Of all the curious! "
she said.

She heard a sniff close behind her head, as it
seemed, and, turning, was surprised to see Hall a
dozen feet off on the topmost stair. But in another
moment he was beside her. She bent forward and
put her hand on the pillow and then under the
clothes.

" Cold," she said. " He's been up this hour or
more."

As she did so a most extraordinary thing happened.
The bed-clothes gathered themselves together, leapt
up suddenly into a sort of peak, and then jumped
headlong over the bottom rail. It was exactly as
if a hand had clutched them in the centre and flung
them aside. Immediately after, the stranger's hat
hopped off the bedpost, described a whirling flight
in the air through the better part of a circle, and
then dashed straight at Mrs. Hall's face. Then as
swiftly came the sponge from the washstand and then
the chair, flinging the stranger's coat and trousers
carelessly aside, and laughing dryly in a voice
singularly like the stranger's, turned itself up with
its four legs at Mrs. Hall, seemed to take aim at her
for a moment, and charged at her. She screamed
and turned, and then the chair legs came gently
but firmly against her back and impelled her and
Hall out of the room. The door slammed violently,
and was locked. The chair and bed seemed to be
executing a dance of triumph for a moment, and
then abruptly everything was still.

Mrs. Hall was left almost in a fainting condition
in Mr. Hall's arms on the landing. It was with the
greatest difficulty that Mr. Hall and Millie, who

had been roused by her scream of alarm, succeeded in getting her downstairs, and applying the restoratives customary in such cases.

" 'Tas sperits," said Mrs. Hall. " I know 'tas sperits. I've read in papers of en. Tables and chairs leaping and dancing . . ."

" Take a drop more, Janny," said Hall. " 'Twill steady ye."

" Lock him out," said Mrs. Hall. " Don't let him come in again. I half guessed . . . I might ha' known. With them goggling eyes and bandaged head, and never going to church of a Sunday. And all they bottles—more'n it's right for anyone to have. He's put the sperits into the furniture. . . . My good old furniture! 'Twas in that very chair my poor dear mother used to sit when I was a little girl. To think it should rise up against me now . . ."

" Just a drop more, Janny," said Hall. " Your nerves is all upset."

They sent Millie across the street through the golden five o'clock sunshine to rouse up Mr. Sandy Wadgers, the blacksmith.

Mr. Hall's compliments, and the furniture upstairs was behaving most extraordinary. Would Mr. Wadgers come round?

He was a knowing man, was Mr. Wadgers, and very resourceful. He took quite a grave view of the case.

"Arm darmed if thet ent witchcraft," was the view of Mr. Sandy Wadgers. " You warnt horseshoes for such gentry as he."

He came round greatly concerned. They wanted him to lead the way upstairs to the room; but he didn't seem to be in any hurry. He preferred to talk in the passage. Over the way Huxter's apprentice came out, and began taking down the shutters of the tobacco window. He was called over to join the discussion. Mr. Huxter naturally followed in the course of a few minutes. The Anglo-Saxon genius for parliamentary government asserted itself: there was a great deal of talk and no decisive action.

" Let's have the facts first," insisted Mr. Sandy Wadgers. " Let's be sure we'd be acting perfectly right in bustin' that there door open. A door onbust is always open to bustin', but ye can't onbust a bust door once you've busted en."

And suddenly and most wonderfully the door of the room upstairs opened of its own accord, and as they looked up in amazement, they saw descending the stairs the muffled figure of the stranger, staring more blackly and blankly than ever with those unreasonably large glass eyes of his. He came down stiffly and slowly, staring all the time; he walked across the passage, staring, then stopped.

" Look there! " he said, and their eyes followed the direction of his gloved finger, and saw a bottle of sarsaparilla hard by the cellar door. Then he entered the parlour, and suddenly, swiftly, viciously, slammed the door in their faces.

Not a word was spoken until the last echoes of the slam had died away. They stared at one another.

" Well, if that don't lick everything! " said Mr. Wadgers, and left the alternative unsaid.

" I'd go in and ask'n 'bout it," said Wadgers to Mr. Hall. " I'd d'mand an explanation."

It took some time to bring the landlady's husband up to that pitch.

At last he rapped, opened the door, and got as far as:

" Excuse me——"

" Go to the devil! " said the stranger in a tremendous voice, and, " Shut that door after you."

So this brief interview terminated.

7

The Unveiling of the Stranger

THE stranger went into the little parlour of the " Coach and-Horses " about half-past five in the morning, and there he remained until near midday, the blinds down, the door shut, and none, after Hall's repulse, venturing near him.

All that time he must have fasted. Thrice he rang his bell, the third time furiously and continuously, but no one answered him. " Him and his ' Go to the devil,' indeed! " said Mrs. Hall. Presently came an imperfect rumour of the burglary at the Vicarage, and two and two were put together. Hall, assisted by Wadgers, went off to find Mr. Shuckleforth, the magistrate, and take his advice. No one ventured upstairs. How the stranger occupied himself is unknown. Now and then he would stride violently up and down, and twice came an outburst of curses, a tearing of paper, and a violent smashing of bottles.

The little group of scared but curious people increased. Mrs. Huxter came over; some gay young fellows resplendent in black, ready-made jackets and *pique* paper ties—for it was Whit Monday —joined the group with confused and confusing interrogations. Young Archie Harker distinguished himself by going up the yard and trying to peep under the drawn blinds. He could see nothing, but

gave reason for supposing that he did, and others
of the Iping youth presently joined him.

It was the finest of all possible Whit Mondays,
and down the village street stood a row of nearly a
dozen booths, a shooting-gallery, and on the grass
by the forge were three yellow and chocolate wagons,
and some picturesque strangers of both sexes putting
up a coconut shy. The gentlemen wore blue jerseys,
the ladies white aprons and quite fashionable hats
with heavy plumes.   Woodyer, of the " Purple
Fawn," and Mr. Jaggers, the cobbler, who also sold
second-hand ordinary bicycles, were stretching a
string of union jacks and royal ensigns, which had
originally celebrated the first Victorian Jubilee,
across the road.

And inside in the artificial darkness of the parlour,
into which only one thin jet of sunlight penetrated,
the stranger, hungry we must suppose, and fearful,
hidden in his uncomfortable hot wrappings, pored
through his dark glasses upon his paper, or chinked
his dirty little bottles, and occasionally swore
savagely at the boys, audible, if invisible, outside
the windows. In the corner by the fireplace lay the
fragments of half a dozen smashed bottles, and a
pungent twang of chlorine tainted the air. So much
we know from what was heard at the time, and from
what was subsequently seen in the room.

About noon he suddenly opened his parlour door
and stood glaring fixedly at the three or four people
in the bar. " Mrs. Hall," he said. Somebody went
sheepishly and called for Mrs. Hall.

Mrs. Hall appeared after an interval, a little short
of breath, but all the fiercer for that. Hall was still
out. She had deliberated over this scene, and she

came holding a little tray with an unsettled bill upon it. " Is it your bill you're wanting, sir? " she said.

" Why wasn't my breakfast laid? Why haven't you prepared my meals and answered my bell? Do you think I live without eating? "

" Why isn't my bill paid? " said Mrs. Hall. " That's what I want to know."

" I told you three days ago I was awaiting a remittance——"

" I told you three days ago I wasn't going to await no remittances. You can't grumble if your breakfast waits a bit, if my bill's been waiting these five days, can you? "

The stranger swore briefly but vividly.

" Nar, nar! " from the bar.

" And I'd thank you kindly, sir, if you'd keep your swearing to yourself, sir," said Mrs. Hall.

The stranger stood looking more like an angry diving helmet than ever. It was universally felt in the bar that Mrs. Hall had the better of him. His next words showed as much.

" Look here, my good woman——" he began.

" Don't ' good woman ' *me*," said Mrs. Hall.

" I've told you my remittance hasn't come."

" Remittance, indeed! " said Mrs. Hall.

" Still, I dare say in my pocket——"

" You told me three days ago that you hadn't anything but a sovereign's worth of silver upon you."

" Well, I've found some more."

" 'Ul-*lo*! " from the bar.

" I wonder where you found it? " said Mrs. Hall. That seemed to annoy the stranger, very much.

He stamped his foot. "What do you mean?" he said.

"That I wonder where you found it," said Mrs. Hall. "And before I take any bills, or get any breakfasts, or do any such things whatsoever, you got to tell me one or two things I don't understand, and what nobody don't understand, and what everybody is very anxious to understand. I want to know what you been doing t'my chair upstairs, and I want to know how 'tis your room was empty and how you got in again? Them as stops in this house comes in by the doors—that's the rule of this house, and that you *didn't* do, and what I want to know is how you *did* come. And I want to know——"

Suddenly the stranger raised his gloved hands clenched, stamped his foot, and said, "Stop!" with such extraordinary violence that he silenced her instantly.

"You don't understand," he said, "who I am or what I am. I'll show you. By heaven! I'll show you." Then he put his open palm over his face and withdrew it. The centre of his face became a black cavity. "Here," he said. He stepped forward and handed Mrs. Hall something which she, staring at his metamorphosed face, accepted automatically. Then, when she saw what it was, she screamed loudly, dropped it, and staggered back. The nose —it was the stranger's nose! pink and shining— rolled on the floor with a sound of hollow cardboard.

Then he removed his spectacles, and everyone in the bar gasped. He took off his hat, and with a violent gesture tore at his whiskers and bandages. For a moment they resisted him. A flash of horrible

3   I.M.

anticipation passed through the bar. "Oh, my Gard!" said someone. Then off they came.

It was worse than anything. Mrs. Hall, standing open-mouthed and horror-struck, shrieked at what she saw, and made for the door of the house. Everyone began to move. They were prepared for scars, disfigurement, tangible horrors—but *nothing*! The bandages and false hair flew across the passage into the bar, making a hobbledehoy jump to avoid them. Everyone tumbled on everyone else down the steps. For the man who stood there shouting some incoherent explanation was a solid, gesticulating figure up to the coat-collar of him, and then—nothingness, no visible thing at all!

People down the village heard shouts and shrieks, and looking up the street saw the "Coach and Horses" violently firing out its humanity. They saw Mrs. Hall fall down, and Mr. Teddy Henfrey jump to avoid tumbling over her, and then they heard the frightful screams of Millie, who, emerging suddenly from the kitchen at the noise of the tumult, had come upon the headless stranger from behind. These ceased suddenly.

Forthwith everyone all the way down the street —the sweetstuff-seller, coconut-shy proprietor and his assistant, the swing man, little boys and girls, rustic dandies, smart wenches, smocked elders, and aproned gipsies—began running towards the inn, and in a miraculously short space of time a crowd of perhaps forty people, and rapidly increasing, swayed, and hooted, and inquired, and exclaimed, and suggested in front of Mrs. Hall's establishment. Everybody seemed eager to talk at once, and the result was Babel. A small group supported Mrs.

Hall, who was picked up in a state of collapse. There was a confusion, and the incredible evidence of a vociferous eye-witness. " O Bogie." " What's he been doin', then?" " Ain't hurt the girl, 'as 'e?" " Run at en with a knife, I believe." " No 'ed, I tell ye. I don't mean no manner of speaking, I mean Marn 'ithout a 'Ed!" " Narnsense! 'tis some conjuring trick." " Fetched off 'is wrappings, 'e did——"

In its struggles to see in through the open door the crowd formed itself into a struggling wedge, with the more adventurous apex nearest the inn. " He stood for a moment, I heerd the gal scream, and he turned. I saw her skirts whisk, and he went after her. Didn't take ten seconds. Back he comes with a knife in his hand and a loaf, stood just as if he was staring. Not a moment ago. Went in that there door. I tell 'e, 'e ain't gart no 'd 'tall. You just missed en——"

There was a disturbance behind, and the speaker stopped to step aside for a little procession that was marching very resolutely towards the house; first Mr. Hall, very red and determined, then Mr. Bobby Jaffers, the village constable, and then the wary Mr. Wadgers. They had come now armed with a warrant.

People shouted conflicting information of the recent circumstances. " 'Ed or no 'ed," said Jaffers. " I got to 'rest en, and 'rest en I *will*."

Mr. Hall marched up the steps, marched straight to the door of the parlour and found it open. " Constable," he said, " do your duty."

Jaffers marched in, Hall next, Wadgers last. They saw in the dim light the headless figure facing them, with a gnawed crust of bread in one gloved hand and a chunk of cheese in the other.

" That's him," said Hall.

" What the devil's this? " came in a tone of angry expostulation from above the collar of the figure.

" You're a darned rum customer, mister," said Mr. Jaffers. " But 'ed or no 'ed, the warrant says ' body,' and duty's duty——"

" Keep off! " said the figure, starting back.

Abruptly he whipped down the bread and cheese, and Mr. Hall just grasped the knife on the table in time to save it. Off came the stranger's left glove, and was slapped in Jaffer's face. In another moment Jaffers, cutting short some statement concerning a warrant, had gripped him by the handless wrist, and caught his invisible throat. He got a sounding kick on the shin that made him shout, but he kept his grip. Hall sent the knife sliding along the table to Wadgers, who acted as goal-keeper for the offensive, so to speak, and then stepped forward as Jaffers and the stranger swayed and staggered towards him, clutching and hitting in. A chair stood in the way, and went aside with a crash as they came down together.

" Get the feet," said Jaffers between his teeth.

Mr. Hall, endeavouring to act on instructions, received a sounding kick in the ribs that disposed of him for a moment; and Mr. Wadgers, seeing the decapitated stranger had rolled over and got the upper side of Jaffers, retreated towards the door, knife in hand, and so collided with Mr. Huxter and the Sidderbridge carter coming to the rescue of law and order. At the same moment down came three or four bottles from the chiffonier and shot a web of pungency into the air of the room.

"I'll surrender," cried the stranger, though he had Jaffers down, and in another moment he stood up panting, a strange figure, headless and handless —for he had pulled off his right glove now as well as his left. "It's no good," he said, as if sobbing for breath.

It was the strangest thing in the world to hear that voice coming as if out of empty space, but the Sussex peasants are perhaps the most matter-of-fact people under the sun. Jaffers got up also, and produced a pair of handcuffs. Then he stared.

"I say!" said Jaffers, brought up short by a dim realisation of the incongruity of the whole business. "Darm it! Can't use 'em as I can see."

The stranger ran his arm down his waistcoat, and, as if by a miracle, the buttons to which his empty sleeve pointed became undone. Then he said something about his shin, and stooped down. He seemed to be fumbling with his shoes and socks.

"Why!" said Huxter suddenly, "that's not a man at all. It's just empty clothes. Look! You can see down his collar and the linings of his clothes. I could put my arm——"

He extended his hand; it seemed to meet something in mid-air, and he drew it back with a sharp exclamation. "I wish you'd keep your fingers out of my eye," said the aerial voice in a tone of savage expostulation. "The fact is, I'm all here—head, hands, legs, and all the rest of it, but it happens I'm invisible. It's a confounded nuisance, but I am. That's no reason why I should be poked to pieces by every stupid bumpkin in Iping, is it?"

The suit of clothes, now all unbuttoned and hanging loosely upon its unseen supports, stood up, arms akimbo.

Several other of the men folk had now entered the room, so that it was closely crowded. " Invisible, eh? " said Huxter, ignoring the stranger's abuse. " Who ever heard the likes of that? "

" It's strange, perhaps, but it's not a crime. Why am I assaulted by a policeman in this fashion——"

" Ah! that's a different matter," said Jaffers. " No doubt you are a bit difficult to see in this light, but I got a warrant and it's all correct. What I'm after ain't no invisibility, it's burglary. There's a house been broke into, and money took."

" Well? "

" And circumstances certainly point——"

" Stuff and nonsense! " said the Invisible Man.

" I hope so, sir. But I've got my instructions——"

" Well," said the stranger, " I'll come. I'll *come*. But no handcuffs."

" It's the regular thing," said Jaffers.

" No handcuffs," stipulated the stranger.

" Pardon me," said Jaffers.

Abruptly the figure sat down, and before any one could realise what was being done, the slippers, socks, and trousers had been kicked off under the table. Then he sprang up again and flung off his coat

" Here, stop that," said Jaffers, suddenly realising what was happening. He gripped the waistcoat, it struggled, and the shirt slipped out of it and left it limp and empty in his hand. " Hold him! " said Jaffers loudly. " Once he gets the things off——"

" Hold him! " cried everyone, and there was a

rush at the fluttering white shirt, which was now all that was visible of the stranger.

The shirt sleeve planted a shrewd blow in Hall's face that stopped his open-armed advance and sent him backward into old Toothsome, the sexton, and in another moment the garment was lifted up, and became convulsed and vacantly flapping about the arms, even as a shirt that is being thrust off over a man's head. Jaffers clutched at it, and only helped to pull it off. He was struck in the mouth out of the air, and incontinently drew his truncheon and smote Teddy Henfrey savagely upon the crown of his head.

"Look out!" said everybody, fencing at random and hitting at nothing. "Hold him! Shut the door! Don't let him loose. I got something! Here he is!" A perfect Babel of noises they made. Everybody, it seemed, was being hit all at once, and Sandy Wadgers, knowing as ever, and his wits sharpened by a frightful blow on the nose, reopened the door and led the rout. The others, following incontinently, were jammed for a moment in the corner by the doorway. The hitting continued. Phipps, the Unitarian, had a front tooth broken, and Henfrey was injured in the cartilage of his ear. Jaffers was struck under the jaw, and, turning, caught at something that intervened between him and Huxter in the *mêlée*, and prevented their coming together. He felt a muscular chest, and in another moment the whole mass of struggling, excited men shot out into the crowded hall.

"I got him!" shouted Jaffers, choking and reeling through them all, and wrestling with purple face and swelling veins against his unseen enemy.

Men staggered right and left as the extraordinary conflict swayed swiftly towards the house door and went spinning down the half dozen steps of the inn. Jaffers cried in a strangled voice, holding tight nevertheless, and making play with his knee, spun round and fell heavily undermost with his head on the gravel. Only then did his fingers relax.

There were excited cried of " Hold him! " " Invisible! " and so forth, and a young fellow, a stranger in the place, whose name did not come to light, rushed in at once, caught something, missed his hold, and fell over the constable's prostrate body. Half-way across the road a woman screamed as something pushed by her, a dog, kicked apparently, yelped and ran howling into Huxter's yard, and with that the transit of the Invisible Man was accomplished. For a space people stood amazed and gesticulating, and then came panic, and scattered them abroad through the village as a gust scatters dead leaves. But Jaffers lay quite still, face and knees upward bent, at the foot of the steps of the inn.

8

In Transit

THE eighth chapter is exceedingly brief, and relates
that Gibbins, the amateur naturalist of the district,
while lying out on the spacious open downs without
a soul within a couple of miles of him as he thought,
and almost dozing, heard close to him the sound
as of a man coughing, sneezing, and then swearing
savagely to himself, and looking, beheld nothing.
Yet the voice was indisputable. It contined to swear
with that breadth and variety that distinguishes the
swearing of a cultivated man. It grew to a climax,
diminished again and died away in the distance,
going, as it seemed to him, in the direction of
Adderdean. It lifted to a spasmodic sneeze, and
ended. Gibbins had heard nothing of the morning's
occurrences, but the phenomenon was so striking
and disturbing, that his philosophical tranquillity
vanished; he got up hastily and hurried down the
steepness of the hill, towards the village, as fast as
he could go.

9

Mr. Thomas Marvel

You must picture Mr. Thomas Marvel as a person of copious, flexible visage, a nose of cylindrical protrusion, a liquorish, ample, fluctuating mouth, and a beard of bristling eccentricity. His figure inclined to *embonpoint*, his short limbs accentuated this inclination. He wore a furry silk hat, and the frequent substitution of twine and shoe-laces for buttons, apparent at critical points of his costume, marked a man essentially bachelor.

Mr. Thomas Marvel was sitting with his feet in a ditch by the roadside over the down towards Adderdean, about a mile and a half out of Iping. His feet, save for socks of irregular open-work, were bare, his big toes were broad, and pricked like the ears of a watchful dog. In a leisurely manner—he did everything in a leisurely manner—he was contemplating a pair of lace-up boots. They were the soundest boots he had come across for a long time, but too large for him, whereas those he had had were, in dry weather, a very comfortable fit, but too thin soled for damp. Mr. Thomas Marvel hated roomy boots, but then he hated damp. He had never properly thought out which he hated most, and it was a pleasant day, and there was nothing better to do. So he put the four boots in a graceful group on the turf, and looked at them.

And seeing them there among the grass and spring-ing agrimony, it suddenly occurred to him that both pairs were exceedingly ugly to see. He was not at all startled by a voice behind him.

" They're boots, anyhow," said the Voice.

" They are—Charity Boots," said Mr. Thomas Marvel, with his head on one side regarding them distastefully; " and which is the ugliest pair in the whole blessed universe, I'm darned if I know! "

" H'm," said the Voice.

" I've worn worse—in fact, I've worn none. But none so owdacious ugly—if you'll allow the ex-pression. I've been cadging boots—in particular—for days, because I was sick of *them.* They're sound enough, of course. But a gentleman on tramp sees such a thundering lot of his boots. And if you'll believe me, I've raised nothing in the whole blessed county, try as I would, but *them.* Look at 'em! And a good county for boots, too, in a general way. But it's just my promiscuous luck. I've got my boots in this county ten years or more. And then they treat you like this."

" It's a beast of a county," said the Voice, " and pigs for people."

" Ain't it? " said Mr. Thomas Marvel. " Lord! But them boots! It beats it."

He turned his head over his shoulder to the right, to look at the boots of his interlocutor, with a view to comparisons, and lo! where the boots of his interlocutor should have been were neither legs nor boots. He turned his head over his shoulder to the left, and there also were neither legs nor boots. He was irradiated by the dawn of a great amazement. "Where *are* yer?" said Mr. Thomas Marvel over his shoulder, and coming on all fours. He saw a stretch of empty down, with the wind swaying the remote green-pointed furze bushes.

" Am I drunk? " said Mr. Marvel. " Have I had visions? Was I talking to myself? What the——"

" Don't be alarmed," said a Voice.

" None of your ventriloquising *me*," said Mr. Thomas Marvel, rising sharply to his feet. " Where *are* yer? Alarmed, indeed! "

" Don't be alarmed," repeated the Voice.

" *You'll* be alarmed in a minute, you silly fool," said Mr. Thomas Marvel. " Where *are* yer? Lemme get my mark on yer . . .

" Are yer *buried*? " said Mr. Thomas Marvel after an interval.

There was no answer. Mr. Thomas Marvel stood bootless and amazed, his jacket nearly thrown off.

" Peewit," said a peewit very remote.

" Peewit, indeed! " said Mr. Thomas Marvel. " This ain't no time for foolery." The down was desolate east and west, north and south; the road, with its shallow ditches and white bordering stakes, ran smooth and empty north and south, and, save for that peewit, the blue sky was empty too. " So help me," said Mr. Thomas Marvel, shuffling his coat on to his shoulders again. " It's the drink. I might ha' known."

" It's not the drink," said the Voice. " You keep your nerves steady."

" Ow! " said Mr. Marvel, and his face grew white amidst its patches. " It's the drink," his lips repeated noiselessly. He remained staring about him, rotating slowly backwards. " I could have *swore* I heard a voice," he whispered.

" Of course you did."

" It's there again," said Mr. Marvel, closing his eyes and clasping his hand on his brow with a tragic gesture. He was suddenly taken by the collar and shaken violently, and left more dazed than ever. " Don't be a fool! " said the Voice.

" I'm—off—my—blooming chump! " said Mr. Marvel. " It's no good. It's fretting about them blarsted boots. I'm off my blessed, blooming chump. Or it's spirits! "

" Neither one thing nor the other," said the Voice. " Listen! "

" Chump! " said Mr. Marvel.

" One minute," said the Voice penetratingly, tremulous with self-control.

" Well? " said Mr. Thomas Marvel, with a strange feeling of having been dug in the chest by a finger.

" You think I'm just imagination—just imagination? "

" What else *can* you be? " said Mr. Thomas Marvel, rubbing the back of his neck.

" Very well," said the Voice in a tone of relief. " Then I'm going to throw flints at you till you think differently."

" But where *are* yer? "

The Voice made no answer. Whizz came a flint, apparently out of the air, and missed Mr. Marvel's shoulder by a hair's breadth. Mr. Marvel, turning, saw a flint jerk up into the air, trace a complicated path, hang for a moment, and then fall at his feet with almost invisible rapidity. He was too amazed to dodge. Whizz it came, and ricocheted from a bare toe into the ditch. Mr. Thomas Marvel jumped a foot, and howled aloud. Then he started to run, tripped over an unseen obstacle, and came head over heels into a sitting position.

"*Now*," said the Voice, as a third stone curved upward and hung in the air above the tramp, "am I imagination?"

Mr. Marvel, by way of reply, struggled to his feet, and was immediately rolled over again. He lay quiet for a moment.

"If you struggle any more," said the Voice, "I shall throw the flint at your head."

"It's a fair do," said Mr. Thomas Marvel, sitting up, taking his wounded toe in hand, and fixing his eye on the third missile. "I don't understand it. Stones flinging themselves. Stones talking. Put yourself down. Rot away. I'm done."

The third flint fell.

"It's very simple," said the Voice. "I'm an invisible man."

"Tell us something I don't know," said Mr. Marvel, gasping with pain. "Where you've hid—how you do it—I *don't* know. I'm beat."

"That's all," said the Voice. "I'm invisible. That's what I want you to understand."

"Anyone could see that. There is no need for you to be so confounded impatient, mister. *Now*, then. Give us a notion. How are you hid?"

"I'm invisible. That's the great point. And what I want you to understand is this——"

"But whereabouts?" interrupted Mr. Marvel.

"Here—six yards in front of you."

"Oh, *come*! I ain't blind. You'll be telling me next you're just thin air. I'm not one of your ignorant tramps——"

" Yes. I am—thin air. You're looking through me."

" What! Ain't there any stuff to you? *Vox et*— what is it?—jabber. Is it that? "

" I am just a human being—solid, needing food and drink, needing covering, too. . . . But I'm invisible. You see? Invisible. Simple idea. Invisible."

" What, real like? "

" Yes, real."

" Let's have a hand of you," said Marvel, " if you *are* real. It won't be so darn out-of-the-way like, then——

" *Lord!* " he said, " how you made me jump!— gripping me like that! "

He felt the hand that had closed round his wrist with his disengaged fingers, and his touch went timorously up the arm, patted a muscular chest, and explored a bearded face. Marvel's face was astonishment.

" I'm dashed! " he said. " If this don't beat cock-fighting! Most remarkable!—And there I can see a rabbit clean through you arf a mile away! Not a bit of you visible—cxccpt——"

He scrutinised the apparently empty space keenly.

" You 'aven't been eatin' bread and cheese? " he asked, holding the invisible arm.

" You are quite right. It's not assimilated into the system."

" Ah! " said Mr. Marvel. " Sort of ghostly, though."

" Of course, all this isn't half so wonderful as you think."

"It's quite wonderful enough for *my* modest wants," said Mr. Thomas Marvel. "Howjer manage it? How the dooce is it done?"

"It's too long a story. And besides——"

"I tell you, the whole business fair beats me," said Mr. Marvel.

"What I want to say at present is this: I need help. I have come to that. I came upon you suddenly. I was wandering, mad with rage, naked, impotent. I could have murdered. . . . And I saw you——"

"*Lord!*" said Mr. Marvel.

"I came up behind you—hesitated—went on."

Mr. Marvel's expression was eloquent.

"Then stopped. 'Here,' I said, 'is an outcast like myself. This is the man for me.' So I turned back and came to you. You. And——"

"*Lord!*" said Mr. Marvel. "But I'm all in a dizzy. May I ask: How is it?—and what you may be requiring in the way of help? Invisible!"

"I want you to help me get clothes and shelter, and then with other things. I've left them long enough. If you won't—well! . . . But you *will—must.*"

"Look here," said Mr. Marvel. "I'm too flabbergasted. Don't knock me about any more. And leave me go. I must get steady a bit. And you've pretty near broken my toe. It's all so unreasonable. Empty downs, empty sky. Nothing visible for miles except the bosom of Nature. And then comes a voice. A voice out of heaven! And stones. And a fist. Lord!"

"Pull yourself together," said the Voice, "for you have to do the job I've chosen for you."

Mr. Marvel blew out his cheeks, and his eyes were round.

"I've chosen you," said the Voice. "You are the only man, except some of those fools down there, who knows there is such a thing as an Invisible Man. You have to be my helper. Help me—and I will do great things for you. An Invisible Man is a man of power." He stopped for a moment to sneeze violently.

"But if you betray me," he said, "if you fail to do as I direct you——"

He paused and tapped Mr. Marvel's shoulder smartly. Mr. Marvel gave a yelp of terror at the touch. "I don't want to betray you," said Mr. Marvel, edging away from the direction of the fingers. "Don't you go a-thinking that, whatever you do. All I want to do is to help you—just tell me what I got to do. (Lord!) Whatever you want done, that I'm most willing to do."

10

Mr. Marvel's Visit to Iping

AFTER the first gusty panic had spent itself, Iping
became argumentative. Scepticism suddenly
reared its head—rather nervous scepticism, not at all
assured of its back, but scepticism nevertheless. It
is so much easier not to believe in an Invisible Man,
and those who had actually seen him dissolve into
air or felt the strength of his arm could be counted
on the fingers of two hands. And of these witnesses,
Mr. Wadgers was presently missing, having retired
impregnably behind the bolts and bars of his own
house, and Jaffers was lying stunned in the parlour
of the " Coach and Horses." Great and strange
ideas transcending experience often have less effect
upon men and women than smaller, more tangible
considerations. Iping was gay with bunting, and
everybody was in gala dress. Whit Monday had
been looked forward to for a month or more. By
the afternoon even those who believed in the Unseen
were beginning to resume their little amusements
in a tentative fashion, on the supposition that he had
quite gone away, and with the sceptics he was
already a jest. But people—sceptics and believers
alike—were remarkably sociable all that day.

Haysman's meadow was gay with a tent, in which
Mrs. Bunting and other ladies were preparing tea,
while without the Sunday school children ran races
and played games under the noisy guidance of the

curate and the Misses Cuss and Sackbut. No doubt there was a slight uneasiness in the air, but people for the most part had the sense to conceal whatever imaginative qualms they experienced. On the village green an inclined string, down which, clinging the while to a pulley-swung handle, one could be hurled violently against a sack at the other end, came in for considerable favour among the adolescent, as also did the swings and the coconut-shies. There was also promenading, and the steam organ attached to a small roundabout filled the air with a pungent flavour of oil and with equally pungent music. Members of the club, who had attended church in the morning, were splendid in badges of pink and green, and some of the gayer minded had also adorned their bowler hats with brilliant coloured favours of ribbon. Old Fletcher, whose conceptions of holiday-making were severe, was visible through the jasmine about his window or through the open door (whichever way you chose to look) poised delicately on a plank supported on two chairs, and whitewashing the ceiling of his front room.

About four o'clock a stranger entered the village from the direction of the downs. He was a short, stout person in an extraordinarily shabby top hat, and he appeared to be very much out of breath. His cheeks were alternately limp and tightly puffed. His mottled face was apprehensive, and he moved with a sort of reluctant alacrity. He turned the corner by the church and directed his way to the "Coach and Horses." Among others, old Fletcher remembers seeing him, and indeed the old gentleman was so struck by his peculiar agitation that he inadvertently allowed a quantity of whitewash to run down the brush into the sleeve of his coat while regarding him.

This stranger, to the perceptions of the proprietor of the coconut-shy, appeared to be talking to himself, and Mr. Huxter remarked the same thing. He stopped at the foot of the " Coach and Horses " steps, and, according to Mr. Huxter, appeared to undergo a severe internal struggle before he could induce himself to enter the house. Finally he marched up the steps, and was seen by Mr. Huxter to turn to the left and open the door of the parlour. Mr. Huxter heard voices from within the room and from the bar apprising the man of his error.

" That room's private! " said Hall, and the stranger shut the door clumsily and went into the bar.

In the course of a few minutes he reappeared, wiping his lips with the back of his hand, with an air of quiet satisfaction that somehow impressed Mr. Huxter as assumed. He stood looking about him for some moments, and then Mr. Huxter saw him walk in an oddly furtive manner towards the gates of the yard, upon which the parlour window opened. The stranger, after some hesitation, leant against one of the gate-posts, produced a short clay pipe, and prepared to fill it. His fingers trembled while doing so. He lit it clumsily, and, folding his arms, began to smoke in a languid attitude, an attitude which his occasional quick glances up the yard altogether belied.

All this Mr. Huxter saw over the canisters of the tobacco window, and the singularity of the man's behaviour prompted him to maintain his observation.

Presently the stranger stood up abruptly and put his pipe in his pocket. Then he vanished into the yard. Forthwith Mr. Huxter, conceiving he was witness of some petty larceny, leapt round his counter and ran out into the road to intercept the thief. As he did so, Mr. Marvel reappeared, his hat askew, a big bundle in a blue tablecloth in one hand, and three books tied together—as it proved afterwards with the vicar's braces—in the other. Directly he saw Huxter he gave a sort of gasp, and turning sharply to the left, began to run. "Stop thief!" cried Huxter, and set off after him.

Mr. Huxter's sensations were vivid but brief. He saw the man just before him, and sprinting briskly for the church corner and the down road. He saw the village flags and festivities beyond, and only a face or two turned toward him. He bawled, "Stop thief" again, and set off gallantly. He had hardly gone ten strides before his shin was caught in some mysterious fashion, and he was no longer running but flying with incredible velocity through the air. He saw the ground suddenly close to his head. The world seemed to splash into a million whirling specks of light, and "subsequent proceedings interested him no more."

II

In the " Coach and Horses "

Now, in order to understand clearly what had happened in the inn, it is necessary to go back to the moment when Mr. Marvel first came into view of Mr. Huxter's window.

At that precise moment Mr. Cuss and Mr. Bunting were in the parlour. They were seriously investigating the strange occurrences of the morning, and were, with Mr. Hall's permission, making a thorough examination of the Invisible Man's belongings. Jaffers had partially recovered from his fall and had gone home in the charge of his sympathetic friends. The stranger's scattered garments had been removed by Mrs. Hall, and the room tidied up. And on the table under the window, where the stranger had been wont to work, Cuss had hit almost at once on three big books in manuscript labelled " Diary."

" Diary! " said Cuss, putting the three books on the table. " Now, at any rate, we shall learn something." The vicar stood with his hands on the table.

" Diary," repeated Cuss, sitting down, putting two volumes to support the third, and opening it. " H'm—no name on the fly leaf. Bother! . . . Cipher. And figures."

The vicar came round to look over his shoulder.

Cuss turned the pages over with a face suddenly

disappointed. " I'm—dear me! It's all cipher, Bunting."

" There are no diagrams? " asked Mr. Bunting. " No illustrations throwing light——"

" See for yourself," said Mr. Cuss. " Some of it's mathematical, and some of it's Russian or some such language (to judge by the letters) and some of it's Greek. Now the Greek I thought *you*——"

" Of course," said Mr. Bunting, taking out and wiping his spectacles, and feeling suddenly very uncomfortable—for he had no Greek left in his mind worth talking about. " Yes—the Greek, of course, may furnish a clue."

" I'll find you a place."

" I'd rather glance through the volumes first," said Mr. Bunting, still wiping. " A general impression first, Cuss, and *then*, you know, we can go looking for clues."

He coughed, put on his glasses, arranged them fastidiously, coughed again, and wished something would happen to avert the seemingly inevitable exposure. Then he took the volume Cuss handed him in a leisurely manner. And then something did happen.

The door opened suddenly.

Both men started violently, looked round, and were relieved to see a sporadically rosy face beneath a furry silk hat. " Tap? " asked the face, and stood staring.

" No," said both gentlemen at once.

" Over the other side, my man," said Mr. Bunting. " And please shut that door," said Mr. Cuss irritably.

" All right," said the intruder, as it seemed in a

low voice, curiously different from the huskiness of its first inquiry. " Right you are," said the intruder in the former voice. " Stand clear," and he vanished and closed the door.

" A sailor, I should judge," said Mr. Bunting. " Amusing fellows they are. Stand clear, indeed. A nautical term, referring to his getting back out of the room, I suppose."

" I dare say so," said Cuss. " My nerves are all loose to-day. It quite made me jump—the door opening like that."

Mr. Bunting smiled as if he had not jumped. " And now," he said with a sigh, " these books."

" One minute," said Cuss, and went and locked the door. " Now I think we are safe from inter- ruption."

Someone sniffed as he did so.

" One thing is indisputable," said Bunting, drawing up a chair next to that of Cuss. " There certainly have been very strange things happening in Iping during the last few days—very strange. I cannot, of course, believe in this absurd invisibility story——"

" It's incredible," said Cuss, " incredible. But the fact remains that I saw—I certainly saw right down his sleeve——"

" But did you are you sure . . . Suppose a mirror, for instance. . . . Hallucinations are so easily produced. I don't know if you have ever seen a really good conjurer——"

" I won't argue again," said Cuss. " We've thrashed that out, Bunting. And just now there's these books. . . . Ah! here's some of what I take to be Greek! Greek letters, certainly."

He pointed to the middle of the page. Mr.
Bunting flushed slightly, and brought his face nearer,
apparently finding some difficulty with his glasses.
The little man's Greek was of the flimsiest, and he
firmly believed that everyone outside the Church
credited him with a knowledge of Greek and
Hebrew originals. And now—— Should he confess?
Should he vamp? Suddenly he became aware of a
strange feeling at the nape of his neck. He tried
to move his head, and encountered an immovable
resistance.

The feeling was a curious pressure—the grip of a
heavy, firm hand, and it bore his chin irresistibly to
the table. " *Don't move, little men,*" whispered a
voice, " *or I'll brain you both!* "

He looked into the face of Cuss, close to his own,
and saw a horrified reflection of his own sickly
astonishment.

" I'm sorry to handle you roughly," said the
Voice, " but it's unavoidable.

" Since when did you learn to pry into an investigator's private memoranda? " said the Voice,
and two chins struck the table simultaneously, and
two sets of teeth rattled.

" Since when did you learn to invade the private
rooms of a man in misfortune? " and the concussion
was repeated.

" Where have they put my clothes?

" Listen," said the Voice. " The windows are
fastened, and I've taken the key out of the door.
I am a fairly strong man, and I have the poker
handy—besides being invisible. There's not the
slightest doubt that I could kill you both and get
away quite easily if I wanted to—do you understand?

Very well. If I let you go, will you promise not to try any nonsense, and do what I tell you? "

The vicar and the doctor looked at one another, and the doctor pulled a face. " Yes," said Mr. Bunting, and the doctor repeated it. Then the pressure on the necks relaxed, and the doctor and vicar sat up, both very red in the face, and wriggling their heads.

" Please keep sitting where you are," said the Invisible Man. " Here's the poker, you see.

" When I came into this room," continued the Invisible Man, after presenting the poker to the tip of the nose of each of his visitors, " I did not expect to find it occupied; and I expected to find, in addition to my books of memoranda, an outfit of clothing. Where is it? No—don't rise. I can see it's gone. Now just at present, though the days are quite warm enough for an invisible man to run about stark—the evenings are chilly. I want clothing —and other accommodation. And I must also have those three books."

12

The Invisible Man Loses His Temper

I^T is unavoidable that at this point the narrative should break off again, for a certain very painful reason that will presently be apparent. And while these things were going on in the parlour, and while Mr. Huxter was watching Mr. Marvel smoking his pipe against the gate, not a dozen yards away were Mr. Hall and Teddy Henfrey discussing in a state of cloudy puzzlement the one Iping topic.

Suddenly there came a violent thud against the door of the parlour, a sharp cry, and then—silence.

" *Hul*-lo! " said Teddy Henfrey.

" Hul-*lo*! " from the tap.

Mr. Hall took things in slowly but surely. " That's ain't right," he said, and came round from behind the bar towards the parlour door.

He and Teddy approached the door together, with intent faces. Their eyes considered. " Summat wrong," said Hall, and Henfrey nodded agreement. Whiffs of an unpleasant chemical odour met them, and there was a muffled sound of conversation, very rapid and subdued.

" You all raight thur? " asked Hall, rapping.

The muttered conversation ceased abruptly, for a moment silence, then the conversation was resumed in hissing whispers, then a sharp cry of " No! no you don't! " There came a sudden motion and the oversetting of a chair, a brief struggle.

Silence again.

"What the dooce!" exclaimed Henfrey *sotto voce*.

"You—all—raight—thur?" asked Mr. Hall sharply again.

The vicar's voice answered with a curious jerking intonation. "Quite ri-ight. Please don't—interrupt."

"Odd!" said Mr. Henfrey.

"Odd!" said Mr. Hall.

"Says, 'Don't interrupt,'" said Henfrey.

"I heerd'n," said Hall.

"And a sniff," said Henfrey.

They remained listening. The conversation was rapid and subdued. "I *can't*," said Mr. Bunting, his voice rising; "I tell you, sir, I *will* not."

"What was that?" asked Henfrey.

"Says he wi' nart," said Hall. "Warn't speakin' to us, wuz he?"

"Disgraceful!" said Mr. Bunting within.

"'Disgraceful,'" said Mr. Henfrey. "I heard it—*distinct*."

"Who's that speaking now?" asked Henfrey.

"Mr. Cuss, I s'pose," said Hall. "Can you hear—anything?"

Silence. The sounds within indistinct and perplexing.

"Sounds like throwing the tablecloth about," said Hall.

Mrs. Hall appeared behind the bar. Hall made gestures of silence and invitation. This roused Mrs. Hall's wifely opposition.

"What yer listenin' there for, Hall?" she asked.

"Ain't you nothin' better to do—busy day like this?"

Hall tried to convey everything by grimaces and dumb show, but Mrs. Hall was obdurate. She raised her voice. So Hall and Henfrey, rather crestfallen, tiptoed back to the bar, gesticulating, to explain to her.

At first she refused to see anything in what they had heard at all. Then she insisted on Hall keeping silence, while Henfrey told her his story. She was inclined to think the whole business nonsense— perhaps they were just moving the furniture about.

"I heerd'n say 'disgraceful'; *that* I did," said Hall.

"*I* heard that, Mis' Hall," said Henfrey.

"Like as not," began Mrs. Hall.

"Hsh!" said Mr. Teddy Henfrey. "Didn't I hear the window?"

"What window?" asked Mrs. Hall.

"Parlour window," said Henfrey.

Everyone stood listening intently. Mrs. Hall's eyes, directed straight before her, saw, without seeing, the brilliant oblong of the inn door, the road, white and vivid, and Huxter's shop-front blistering in the June sun. Abruptly Huxter's door opened, and Huxter appeared, eyes staring with excitement, arms gesticulating.

"*Yap!*" cried Huxter. "Stop thief!" and he ran obliquely across the oblong towards the yard gates and vanished.

Simultaneously came a tumult from the parlour, and a sound of windows being closed.

Hall, Henfrey, and the human contents of the tap rushed out at once pell-mell into the street. They

saw someone whisk round the corner towards the
down road, and Mr. Huxter executing a complicated
leap in the air that ended on his face and shoulder.
Down the street people were standing astonished or
running towards them.

Mr. Huxter was stunned. Henfrey stopped to
discover this, but Hall and the two labourers from
the tap rushed at once to the corner, shouting
incoherent things, and saw Mr. Marvel vanishing
by the corner of the church wall. They appear to
have jumped to the impossible conclusion that this
was the Invisible Man suddenly become visible,
and set off at once along the lane in pursuit. But
Hall had hardly run a dozen yards before he gave
a loud shout of astonishment and went flying headlong sideways, clutching one of the labourers and
bringing him to the ground. He had been charged
just as one charges a man at football. The second
labourer came round in a circle, stared, and conceiving that Hall had tumbled over of his own
accord, turned to resume the pursuit, only to be
tripped by the ankle just as Huxter had been.
Then as the first labourer struggled to his feet he
was knocked sideways by a blow that might have
felled an ox.

As he went down, the rush from the direction of
the village green came round the corner. The first
to appear was the proprietor of the coconut-shy, a
burly man in a blue jersey. He was astonished to
see the lane empty save for three men sprawling
absurdly on the ground. And then something
happened to his rearmost foot, and he went headlong
and rolled sideways just in time to snare the feet
of his brother and partner, following headlong. The

two were then kicked, knelt on, fallen over, and cursed by quite a number of over-hasty people.

Now, when Hall and Henfrey and the labourers ran out of the house, Mrs. Hall, who had been disciplined by years of experience, remained in the bar next the till. And suddenly the parlour door was opened, and Mr. Cuss appeared, and, without glancing at her, rushed at once down the steps towards the corner. " Hold him! " he cried, " don't let him drop that parcel! You can see him so long as he holds the parcel."

He knew nothing of the existence of Marvel; for the Invisible Man had handed over the books and bundle in the yard. The face of Mr. Cuss was angry and resolute, but his costume was defective —a sort of limp, white kilt that could only have passed muster in Greece. " Hold him! " he bawled. " He's got my trousers!—and every stitch of the vicar's clothes! "

" 'Tend to him in a minute! " he cried to Henfrey as he passed the prostrate Huxter, and coming round the corner to join the tumult was promptly knocked off his feet into an indecorous sprawl. Somebody in full flight trod heavily on his finger. He yelled, struggled to regain his feet, was knocked against and thrown on all fours again, and became aware that he was involved not in a capture but in a rout. Everyone was running back to the village. He rose again, and was hit severely behind the ear. He staggered, and set off back to the " Coach and Horses " forthwith, leaping over the deserted Huxter, who was now sitting up, on his way.

Behind him, as he was half-way up the inn steps,

he heard a sudden yell of rage, rising sharply out of the confusion of cries, and a sounding smack in someone's face. He recognised the voice as that of the Invisible Man, and the note was that of a man suddenly infuriated by a painful blow.

In another moment Mr. Cuss was back in the parlour.

"He's coming back, Bunting!" he said, rushing in. "Save yourself!"

Mr. Bunting was standing in the window, engaged in an attempt to clothe himself in the hearthrug and a *West Surrey Gazette*.

"Who's coming?" he said, so startled that his costume narrowly escaped disintegration.

"Invisible Man!" said Cuss, and rushed to the window. "We'd better clear out from here. He's fighting mad! Mad!"

In another moment he was out in the yard.

"Good heavens!" said Mr. Bunting, hesitating between two horrible alternatives. He heard a frightful struggle in the passage of the inn, and his decision was made. He clambered out of the window, adjusted his costume hastily, and fled up the village as fast as his fat little legs would carry him.

.   .   .   .   .   .

From the moment when the Invisible Man screamed with rage and Mr. Bunting made his memorable flight up the village, it became impossible to give a consecutive account of affairs in Iping. Possibly the Invisible Man's original intention was simply to cover Marvel's retreat with the clothes and books. But his temper, at no time very good, seems to have gone completely at some chance blow, and forthwith he set to smiting and overthrowing for the mere satisfaction of hurting.

You must figure the street full of running figures, of doors slamming, and fights for hiding-places. You must figure the tumult suddenly striking on the unstable equilibrium of old Fletcher's plank and two chairs—with cataclysmal results. You must figure an appalled couple caught dismally in a swing. And then the whole tumultuous rush has passed, and the Iping street, with its gauds and flags, is deserted, save for the still raging unseen, and littered with coconuts, overthrown canvas screens, and the scattered stock-in-trade of a sweetstuff stall. Everywhere there is a sound of closing shutters and shooting bolts, and the only visible humanity is an occasional flitting eye under a raised eyebrow in the corner of a window-pane.

The Invisible Man amused himself for a little while by breaking all the windows in the "Coach and Horses," and then he thrust a street lamp through the parlour window of Mrs. Grogram. He it must have been who cut the telegraph wire to Adderdean just beyond Higgins's cottage on the Adderdean Road. And after that, as his peculiar qualities allowed, he passed out of human perceptions altogether, and he was neither heard, seen, nor felt in Iping any more. He vanished absolutely.

But it was the best part of two hours before any human being ventured out again into the desolation of Iping Street.

13

Mr. Marvel Discusses His Resignation

WHEN the dusk was gathering, and Iping was just beginning to peep timorously forth again upon the shattered wreckage of its Bank Holiday, a short, thickset man in a shabby silk hat was marching painfully through the twilight behind the beech-woods on the road to Bramblehurst. He carried three books, bound together by some sort of ornamental elastic ligature, and a bundle wrapped in a blue tablecloth. His rubicund face expressed consternation and fatigue; he appeared to be in a spasmodic sort of hurry. He was accompanied by a Voice other than his own, and ever and again he winced under the touch of unseen hands.

" If you give me the slip again," said the Voice; " if you attempt to give me the slip again——"

" Lord! " said Mr. Marvel. " That shoulder's a mass of bruises as it is."

" On my honour," said the Voice, " I will kill you."

" I didn't try to give you the slip," said Marvel, in a voice that was not far remote from tears. " I swear I didn't. I didn't know the blessed turning, that was all! How the devil was I to know the blessed turning? As it is, I've been knocked about——"

" You'll get knocked about a great deal more if

you don't mind," said the Voice, and Mr. Marvel abruptly became silent. He blew out his cheeks, and his eyes were eloquent of despair.

" It's bad enough to let these floundering yokels explode my little secret, without *your* cutting off with my books. It's lucky for some of them they cut and ran when they did! Here am I . . . No one knew I was invisible! And now what am I to do? "

" What am *I* to do? " asked Marvel, *sotto voce*.

" It's all about. It will be in the papers! Everybody will be looking for me. Everyone on their guard——"

The Voice broke off into vivid curses and ceased. The despair of Mr. Marvel's face deepened, and his pace slackened.

" Go on," said the Voice.

Mr. Marvel's face assumed a greyish tint between the ruddier patches.

" Don't drop those books, stupid! " said the Voice sharply.

" The fact is," said the Voice, " I shall have to make use of you. . . . You're a poor tool, but I must."

" I'm a *miserable* tool," said Marvel.

" You are," said the Voice.

" I'm the worst possible tool you could have," said Marvel.

" I'm not strong," he said, after a discouraging silence.

" I'm not over strong," he repeated.

" No? "

" And my heart's weak. That little business—

I pulled it through, of course. But, bless you! I could have dropped."

" Well? "

" I haven't the nerve and strength for the sort of thing you want——"

" *I'll* stimulate you."

" I wish you wouldn't. I wouldn't like to mess up your plans, you know. But I might. Out of sheer funk and misery——"

" You'd better not," said the Voice, with quiet emphasis.

" I wish I was dead," said Marvel.

" It ain't justice," he said. " You must admit . . . It seems to me I've a perfect right——"

" *Get* on," said the Voice.

Mr. Marvel mended his pace, and for a time they went in silence again.

" It's devilish hard," said Mr. Marvel.

This was quite ineffectual. He tried another tack.

" What do I make by it? " he began, again in a tone of unendurable wrong.

" Oh! *shut up!* " said the Voice, with sudden amazing vigour. " I'll see to you all right. You do what you're told. You'll do it all right. You're a fool and all that, but you'll do——"

" I tell you, sir, I'm not the man for it. Respectfully—but it *is* so——"

" If you don't shut up I shall twist your wrist again," said the Invisible Man. " I want to think."

Presently two oblongs of yellow light appeared through the trees, and the square tower of a church loomed through the gloaming. " I shall keep my hand on your shoulder," said the Voice, " all through this village. Go straight through and try no foolery. It will be the worse for you if you do."

"I know that," sighed Mr. Marvel, "I know all that."

The unhappy-looking figure in the obsolete silk hat passed up the street of the little village with his burdens, and vanished into the gathering darkness beyond the lights of the windows.

14

At Port Stowe

TEN o'clock the next morning found Mr. Marvel, unshaven, dirty, and travel-stained, sitting with his hands deep in his pockets, looking very weary, nervous, and uncomfortable, and inflating his cheeks at frequent intervals, on the bench outside a little inn on the outskirts of Port Stowe. Beside him were the books, but now they were tied with string. The bundle had been abandoned in the pinewoods beyond Bramblehurst, in accordance with a change in the plans of the Invisible Man. Mr. Marvel sat on the bench, and although no one took the slightest notice of him, his agitation remained at fever heat. His hands would go ever and again to his various pockets with a curious nervous fumbling.

When he had been sitting for the best part of an hour, however, an elderly mariner, carrying a newspaper, came out of the inn and sat down beside him.

"Pleasant day," said the mariner.

Mr. Marvel glanced about him with something very like terror. "Very," he said.

"Just seasonable weather for the time of year," said the mariner, taking no denial.

"Quite," said Mr. Marvel.

The mariner produced a toothpick, and (saving his regard) was engrossed thereby for some minutes. His eyes meanwhile were at liberty to examine Mr.

Marvel's dusty figure and the books beside him. As he had approached Mr. Marvel he had heard a sound like the dropping of coins into a pocket. He was struck by the contrast of Mr. Marvel's appearance with this suggestion of opulence. Thence his mind wandered back again to a topic that had taken a curiously firm hold of his imagination.

"Books?" he said suddenly, noisily finishing with the toothpick.

Mr. Marvel started and looked at them. "Oh, yes," he said. "Yes, they're books."

"There's some ex-traordinary things in books," said the mariner.

"I believe you," said Mr. Marvel.

"And some extra-ordinary things out of 'em," said the mariner.

"True, likewise," said Mr. Marvel. He eyed his interlocutor, and then glanced about him.

"There's some extra-ordinary things in newspapers, for example," said the mariner.

"There are."

"In *this* newspaper," said the mariner.

"Ah!" said Mr. Marvel.

"There's a story," said the mariner, fixing Mr. Marvel with an eye that was firm and deliberate; "there's a story about an Invisible Man, for instance."

Mr. Marvel pulled his mouth askew and scratched his cheek and felt his ears glowing. "What will they be writing next?" he asked faintly. "Ostria or America?"

"Neither," said the mariner. "*Here.*"

"Lord!" said Mr. Marvel, starting.

"When I say *here*," said the mariner to Mr.

Marvel's intense relief, "I don't, of course, mean here in this place, I mean hereabouts."

"An Invisible Man!" said Mr. Marvel. "And what's *he* been up to?"

"Everything," said the mariner, controlling Marvel with his eye, and then amplifying," every— blessed—thing."

"I ain't seen a paper these four days," said Marvel.

"Iping's the place he started at," said the mariner.

"In-*deed*!" said Mr. Marvel.

"He started there. And where he came from nobody don't seem to know. Here it is: ' Pe-cul-iar Story from Iping.' And it says in this paper that the evidence is extra-ordinary strong, extra-ordinary."

"Lord!" said Mr. Marvel.

"But then it's a extra-ordinary story. There is a clergyman and a medical gent witnesses—saw 'im all right and proper—or leastways, didn't see him. He was staying, it says, at the ' Coach an' Horses,' and no one don't seem to have been aware of his misfortune, it says, aware of his misfortune, until in an Alteration in the inn, it says, his bandages on his head was torn off. It was then ob-served that his head was invisible. Attempts were At Once made to secure him, but, casting off his garments, it says, he succeeded in escaping, but not until after a desperate struggle, In Which he had inflicted serious injuries, it says, on our worthy and able constable, Mr. J. A. Jaffers. Pretty straight story, eh? Names and everything."

"Lord!" said Mr. Marvel, looking nervously about him, trying to count the money in his pockets by his unaided sense of touch, and full of a strange and novel idea. " It sounds most astonishing."

" Don't it? Extra-ordinary, *I* call it. Never heard tell of Invisible Men before, I haven't, but nowadays, one hears such a lot of extra-ordinary things— that——"

" That all he did? " asked Marvel, trying to seem at ease.

" It's enough, ain't it? " said the mariner.

" Didn't go Back by any chance? " asked Marvel. " Just escaped, and that's all, eh? "

" All! " said the mariner. " Why!—ain't it enough? "

" Quite enough," said Marvel.

" I should think it was enough," said the mariner. " I should think it was enough."

" He didn't have any pals—it don't say he had any pals, does it? " asked Mr. Marvel, anxious.

" Ain't one of a sort enough for you? " asked the mariner. " No, thank Heaven, as one might say, he didn't."

He nodded his head slowly. " It makes me regular uncomfortable, the bare thought of that chap running about the country!—— He is at present at large, and from certain evidence, it is supposed that he has—taken—*took*, I suppose they mean—the road to Port Stowe. You see we're right *in* it! None of your American wonders this time. And just think of the things he might do! Where'd you be if he took a drop over and above, and had a fancy to go for you? Suppose he wants to rob— who can prevent him? He can trespass, he can burgle, he can walk through a cordon of policemen as easy as me or you could give the slip to a blind man! Easier! For these here blind chaps hear uncommon sharp. I'm told. And wherever there was liquor he fancied——"

"He's got a tremenjous advantage, certainly," said Mr. Marvel. "And—well . . ."

"You're right," said the mariner; "he *has*."

All this time Mr. Marvel had been glancing about him intently, listening for faint footfalls, trying to detect imperceptible movements. He seemed on the point of some great resolution; he coughed behind his hand.

He looked about him again—listened—bent towards the mariner, and lowered his voice.

"The fact of it is, I happen—to know just a thing or two about this Invisible Man. From private sources."

"Oh!" said the mariner. "*You?*"

"Yes," said Mr. Marvel—"me."

"Indeed!" said the mariner. "And may I ask——?"

"You'll be astonished," said Mr. Marvel, behind his hand. "It's tremenjous."

"Indeed!" said the mariner.

"The fact is," began Mr. Marvel eagerly, in a confidential undertone. Suddenly his expression changed marvellously. "Ow!" he said. He rose stiffly in his seat; his face was eloquent of physical suffering. "Wow!" he said.

"What's up?" said the mariner, concerned.

"Toothache," said Mr. Marvel, and put his hand to his ear. He caught hold of his books. "I must be getting on, I think," he said. He edged in a curious way along the seat away from his interlocutor.

" But you was just a-going to tell me about this here Invisible Man," protested the mariner.

Mr. Marvel seemed to consult with himself.

" Hoax," said a Voice.

" It's a hoax," said Mr. Marvel.

" But it's in the paper," said the mariner.

" Hoax all the same," said Marvel. " I know the chap that started the lie. There ain't no Invisible Man whatsoever. . . . Blimey."

" But how 'bout this paper? D'you mean to say——? "

" Not a word of it," said Mr. Marvel stoutly.

The mariner stared, paper in hand. Mr. Marvel jerkily faced about. " Wait a bit," said the mariner, rising and speaking slowly. " D'you mean to say——? "

" I do," said Mr. Marvel.

" Then why did you let me go on and tell you all this Blarsted stuff, then? What d'yer mean by letting a man make a fool of himself like that for, eh? "

Mr. Marvel blew out his cheeks. The mariner was suddenly very red indeed; he clenched his hands. " I been talking here this ten minutes," he said; " and you, you little pot-bellied, leathery-faced son of an old boot, couldn't have the elementary manners——"

" Don't you come bandying words with *me*," said Mr. Marvel.

" Bandying words! I've a jolly good mind——"

" Come up," said a Voice, and Mr. Marvel was suddenly whirled about and started marching off in a curious, spasmodic manner. " You'd better move on," said the mariner. " *Who's* moving on? " said

Mr. Marvel. He was receding obliquely with a curious, hurrying gait, with occasional violent jerks forward. Some way along the road he began a muttered monologue, protests and recriminations.

" Silly devil," said the mariner, legs wide apart, arms akimbo, watching the receding figure. " I'll show you, you silly fool, hoaxing *me*! It's here in the paper! "

Mr. Marvel retorted incoherently, and receding was hidden by a bend in the road; but the mariner still stood magnificent in the midst of the way, until the approach of a butcher's cart dislodged him. Then he turned himself towards Port Stowe. " Full of extra-ordinary fools," he said softly to himself. " Just to take me down a bit—that was his silly game. . . . It's on the paper! "

And there was another extraordinary thing he was presently to hear that had happened quite close to him. And that was a vision of a " fist full of money " (no less) travelling without visible agency, along by the wall at the corner of St. Michael's Lane. A brother mariner had seen this wonderful sight that very morning. He had snatched the money forthwith, and had been knocked headlong, and when he had got to his feet the butterfly money had vanished. Our mariner was in the mood to believe anything, he declared, but that was a bit *too* stiff. Afterwards, however, he began to think things over.

The story of the flying money was true. And all about that neighbourhood, even from the august London and County Banking Company, from the tills of shops and inns—doors standing that sunny weather entirely open—money had been quietly and dexterously making off that day in handfuls and rouleaux, floating quietly along by walls and shady places, dodging quickly from the approaching eyes of men. And it had, though no man had traced it, invariably ended its mysterious flight in the pocket of that agitated gentleman in the obsolete silk hat, sitting outside the little inn on the outskirts of Port Stowe.

It was ten days after—and indeed only when the Burdock story was already old—that the mariner collated these facts and began to understand how near he had been to the wonderful Invisible Man.

15

The Man Who Was Running

IN the early evening time Dr. Kemp was sitting in his study in the belvedere on the hill overlooking Burdock. It was a pleasant little room, with three windows—north, west, and south—and bookshelves crowded with books and scientific publications, and a broad writing-table, and, under the north window, a microscope, glass slips, minute instruments, some cultures, and scattered bottles of reagents. Dr. Kemp's solar lamp was lit, albeit the sky was still bright with the sunset light, and his blinds were up because there was no offence of peering outsiders to require them pulled down. Dr. Kemp was a tall and slender young man, with flaxen hair and a moustache almost white, and the work he was upon would earn him, he hoped, the fellowship of the Royal Society, so highly did he think of it.

And his eye, presently wandering from his work, caught the sunset blazing at the back of the hill that is over against his own. For a minute, perhaps, he sat, pen in mouth, admiring the rich golden colour above the crest, and then his attention was attracted by the little figure of a man, inky black, running over the hill brow towards him. He was a shortish little fellow, and he wore a high hat, and he was running so fast that his legs verily twinkled.

"Another of those asses," said Dr. Kemp. "Like that ass who ran into me this morning round a corner, with his ''Visible Man a-coming, sir!' I can't imagine what possesses people. One might think we were in the thirteenth century."

He got up, went to the window, and stared at the dusky hillside and the dark little figure tearing down it. "He seems in a confounded hurry," said Dr. Kemp, "but he doesn't seem to be getting on. If his pockets were full of lead, he couldn't run heavier.

"Spurted, sir!" said Dr. Kemp.

In another moment the higher of the villas that had clambered up the hill from Burdock had occulted the running figure. He was visible again for a moment, and again and then again, three times between the three detached houses that came next, and then the terrace hid him.

"Asses!" said Dr. Kemp, swinging round on his heel and walking back to his writing-table.

But those who saw the fugitive nearer, and perceived the abject terror on his perspiring face, being themselves in the open roadway, did not share in the doctor's contempt. By the man pounded, and as he ran he chinked like a well-filled purse that is tossed to and fro. He looked neither to the right nor left, but his dilated eyes stared straight down hill to where the lamps were being lit and the people were crowded in the street. And his ill-shaped mouth fell apart, and a glairy foam lay on his lips, and his breath came hoarse and noisy. All he passed stopped and began staring up the road and down, and interrogating one another with an inkling of discomfort for the reason of his haste.

And then presently, far up the hill, a dog playing in the road yelped and ran under a gate, and as they still wondered, something—a wind—a pad,

pad, pad, a sound like a panting breathing, rushed by.

People screamed. People sprang off the pavement. It passed in shouts, it passed by instinct down the hill. They were shouting in the street before Marvel was half-way there. They were bolting into houses and slamming the doors behind them, with the news. He heard it, and made one last desperate spurt. Fear came striding by, rushed ahead of him, and in a moment had seized the town.

"The Invisible Man is coming! *The Invisible Man!*"

weeping, but still clasping the cloak. "Lemme go inside. Lock me in—somewhere. I tell you he's after me. I give him the slip. He said he'd kill me and he will."

"You're safe," said the man with the black beard. "The door's shut. What's it all about?"

"Lemme go inside," said Marvel, and shrieked aloud as a blow suddenly made the fastened door shake. It was followed by a hurried rapping and a

16
In the " Jolly Cricketers "

THE " Jolly Cricketers " is just at the bottom of the hill, where the tram-lines begin. The barman leant his fat red arms on the counter and talked of horses with an anæmic cabman, while a black-bearded man in grey snapped up biscuit and cheese, drank Burton, and conversed in American with a policeman off duty.

"What's the shouting about?" said the anæmic cabman, going off at a tangent, trying to see up the hill over the dirty yellow blind in the low window of the inn. Somebody ran by outside.

"Fire, perhaps," said the barman.

Footsteps approached, running heavily, the door was pushed open violently, and Marvel, weeping and dishevelled, his hat gone, the neck of his coat torn open, rushed in, made a convulsive turn, and attempted to shut the door. It was held half open by a strap.

"Coming!" he bawled, his voice shrieking with terror. "He's coming. The 'Nvisible Man! After me. For Gawd's sake. 'Elp! 'Elp! 'Elp!"

"Shut the doors," said the policeman. "Who's coming? What's the row?" He went to the door, released the strap, and it slammed. The American closed the other door.

"Lemme go inside," said Marvel, staggering and

weeping, but still clutching the books. " Lemme go inside. Lock me in—somewhere. I tell you he's after me. I give him the slip. He said he'd kill me, and he will."

" *You're* safe," said the man with the black beard. " The door's shut. What's it all about? "

" Lemme go inside," said Marvel, and shrieked aloud as a blow suddenly made the fastened door shiver, and was followed by a hurried rapping and a shouting outside.

" Hullo," cried the policeman, " who's there? "

Mr. Marvel began to make frantic dives at panels that looked like doors. " He'll kill me—he's got a knife or something. For Gawd's sake——! "

" Here you are," said the barman. " Come in here." And he held up the flap of the bar.

Mr. Marvel rushed behind the bar as the summons outside was repeated. " Don't open the door," he screamed. " *Please* don't open the door. *Where* shall I hide? "

" This, this Invisible Man, then? " asked the man with the black beard with one hand behind him. " I guess it's about time we saw him."

The window of the inn was suddenly smashed in, and there was a screaming and running to and fro in the street. The policeman had been standing on the settee staring out, craning to see who was at the door. He got down with raised eyebrows. " It's that," he said.

The barman stood in front of the bar-parlour door, which was now locked on Mr. Marvel, stared at the smashed window, and came round to the two other men.

Everything was suddenly quiet. " I wish I had

my truncheon," said the policeman, going irresolutely
to the door. " Once we open, in he comes. There's
no stopping him."

" Don't you be in too much hurry about that
door," said the anæmic cabman anxiously.

" Draw the bolts," said the man with the black
beard, " and if he comes . . ." He showed a revolver
in his hand.

" That won't do," said the policeman, " that's
murder."

" I know what country I'm in," said the man with
the beard. " I'm going to let off at his legs. Draw
the bolts."

" Not with that thing going off behind me," said
the barman, craning over the blind.

" Very well," said the man with the black beard,
and stooping down, revolver ready, drew them
himself. Barman, cabman, and policeman faced
about.

" Come in," said the bearded man in an undertone, standing back and facing the unbolted doors
with his pistol behind him. No one came in, the
door remained closed.

Five minutes afterwards, when a second cabman
pushed his head in cautiously, they were still waiting,
and an anxious face, peered out of the bar-parlour
and supplied information.

" Are all the doors of the house shut? " asked
Marvel. " He's going round—prowling round. He's
as artful as the devil."

" Good Lord! " said the burly barman. " There's
the back! Just watch them doors! I say——! "
He looked about him helplessly. The bar-parlour
door slammed and they heard the key turn. " There's

the yard door and the private door. The yard
door——"

He rushed out of the bar.

In a minute he reappeared with a carving knife
in his hand. "The yard door was open," he said,
and his fat underlip dropped.

"He may be in the house now," said the first
cabman.

"He's not in the kitchen," said the barman.
"There's two women there, and I've stabbed every
inch of it with this little beef slicer. And they don't
think he's come in. They have noticed——"

"Have you fastened it?" asked the first cabman.

"I'm out of frocks," said the barman.

The man with the beard replaced his revolver.
And even as he did so the flap of the bar was shut
down and the bolt clicked, and then with a
tremendous thud the catch of the door snapped and
the bar-parlour door burst open. They heard
Marvel squeal like a caught leveret, and forthwith
they were clambering over the bar to his rescue.
The bearded man's revolver cracked, and the
looking-glass at the back of the parlour starred and
came smashing and tinkling down.

As the barman entered the room, he saw Marvel
curiously crumpled up and struggling against the
door that led to the yard and kitchen. The door
flew open while the barman hesitated, and Marvel
was lugged into the kitchen. There was a scream
and a clatter of pans. Marvel, head down, and
lugging back obstinately, was forced to the kitchen
door, and the bolts were drawn.

The policeman, who had been trying to pass the
barman, rushed in, followed by one of the cabmen,

gripped the wrist of the invisible hand that collared Marvel, was hit in the face and went reeling back. The door opened, and Marvel made a frantic effort to obtain a lodgment behind it. Then the cabman clutched something.

" I got him," said the cabman.

The barman's red hands came clawing at the unseen.

" Here he is! " said the barman.

Mr. Marvel, released, suddenly dropped to the ground, and made an attempt to crawl behind the legs of the fighting men. The struggle blundered round the edge of the door. The voice of the Invisible Man was heard for the first time, yelling out sharply as the policeman trod on his foot. Then he cried out passionately, and his fists flew round like flails. The cabman suddenly whooped and doubled up, kicked under the diaphragm. The doors into the bar-parlour from the kitchen slammed and covered Mr. Marvel's retreat. The men in the kitchen found themselves clutching at and struggling with empty air.

" Where's he gone? " cried the man with the beard. " Out? "

" This way," said the policeman, stepping into the yard and stopping.

A piece of tile whizzed by his head, and smashed among the crockery on the kitchen table.

" I'll show him," shouted the man with the black beard, and suddenly a steel barrel shone over the policeman's shoulder, and five bullets had followed one another into the twilight whence the missile had come. As he fired, the man with the beard moved his hand in a horizontal curve, so that his shots radiated out into the narrow yard like spokes from a wheel.

A silence followed. " Five cartridges," said the man with the black beard. " That's best of all. Four aces and the joker. Get a lantern, someone, and come and feel about for his body."

17

Dr. Kemp's Visitor

D<small>R.</small> K<small>EMP</small> had continued writing in his study until the shots aroused him. Crack, crack, crack, they came one after the other.

"Hullo!" said Dr. Kemp, putting his pen into his mouth again and listening. "Who's letting off revolvers in Burdock? What are the asses at now?"

He went to the south window, threw it up, and leaning out stared down on the network of windows, beaded gas-lamps and shops with black interstices of roof and yard that made up the town at night. "Looks like a crowd down the hill," he said, "by 'The Cricketers,'" and remained watching. Thence his eyes wandered over the town to far away where the ships' lights shone and the pier glowed—a little illuminated, faceted pavilion like a gem of yellow light. The moon in its first quarter hung over the westward hill, and the stars were clear and almost tropically bright.

After five minutes, during which his mind had travelled into a remote speculation of social conditions of the future, and lost itself at last over the time dimension, Dr. Kemp roused himself with a sigh, pulled down the window again, and returned to his writing-desk.

It must have been about an hour after this that the front-door bell rang. He had been writing slackly, and with intervals of abstraction, since the shots. He sat listening. He heard the servant answer the door, and waited for her feet on the staircase, but she did not come. "Wonder what that was?" said Dr. Kemp.

He tried to resume his work, failed, got up, went downstairs from his study to the landing, rang, and called over the balustrade to the housemaid, as she appeared in the hall below. "Was that a letter?" he asked.

"Only a runaway ring, sir," she answered.

"I'm restless to-night," he said to himself. He went back to his study, and this time attacked his work resolutely.

In a little while he was hard at work again, and the only sounds in the room were the ticking of the clock and the subdued shrillness of his quill, hurrying in the very centre of the circle of light his lampshade threw on his table.

It was two o'clock before Dr. Kemp had finished his work for the night. He rose, yawned, and went upstairs to bed. He had already removed his coat and vest, when he noticed that he was thirsty. He took a candle and went down to the dining-room in search of a siphon and whisky.

Dr. Kemp's scientific pursuits had made him a very observant man, and as he re-crossed the hall he noticed a dark spot on the linoleum near the mat at the foot of the stairs. He went on upstairs, and then it suddenly occurred to him to ask himself what the spot on the linoleum might be. Apparently some sub-conscious element was at work. At any rate, he turned with his burden, went back to the hall, put down the siphon and whisky, and, bending down, touched the spot. Without any great surprise, he found it had the stickiness and colour of drying blood.

He took up his burden again, and returned upstairs looking about him and trying to account for the blood spot. On the landing he saw something, and stopped astonished. The door-handle of his room was bloodstained.

He looked at his own hand. It was quite clean, and then he remembered that the door of his room had been open when he came down from his study, and that consequently he had not touched the handle at all. He went straight into his own room, his face quite calm—perhaps a trifle more resolute than usual. His glance, wandering inquisitively, fell on the bed. On the counterpane was a mess of blood, and the sheet had been torn. He had not noticed this when he had entered the room before, because then he had walked straight to the dressing-table. On the farther side the bed-clothes were depressed as if someone had recently been sitting there.

Then he had an odd impression that he had heard a low voice say, " Good heavens!—Kemp! " But Dr. Kemp was no believer in voices.

He stood staring at the tumbled sheets. Was that really a voice? He looked about again, but noticed nothing further than the disordered and blood-stained bed. Then he distinctly heard a movement across the room, near the washhand-stand. All men, however highly educated, retain some superstitious inklings. The feeling that is called " eerie " came upon him. He closed the door of the room, came forward to the dressing-table, and put down his burden. Suddenly, with a start, he perceived a coiled and blood-stained bandage of linen rag hanging in mid-air, between him and the washhand-stand.

He stared at this in amazement. It was an empty bandage—a bandage properly tied, but quite empty. He would have advanced to grasp it, but a touch arrested him and a voice speaking quite close to him.

" Kemp! " said the Voice.

" Eh? " said Kemp, with his mouth open.

" Keep your nerve," said the Voice. " I'm an Invisible Man."

Kemp made no answer for a space, simply stared at the bandage. " Invisible Man? " he said.

" I am an Invisible Man," repeated the Voice.

The story he had been active to ridicule only that morning rushed through Kemp's brain. He does not appear to have been either very much frightened or very greatly surprised at the moment. Realisation came later.

" I thought it was all a lie," he said. The thought uppermost in his mind was the reiterated arguments of the morning. " Have you a bandage on? " he asked.

" Yes," said the Invisible Man.

" Oh! " said Kemp, and then roused himself. " I say! " he said. " But this is nonsense. It's some trick." He stepped forward suddenly and his hand extended towards the bandage met invisible fingers.

He recoiled at the touch, and his colour changed.

" Keep steady, Kemp, for God's sake! I want help badly. Stop! "

The hand gripped his arm. He struck at it.

" Kemp! " cried the Voice. " Kemp, keep steady! " and the grip tightened.

A frantic desire to free himself took possession of Kemp. The hand of the bandaged arm gripped his shoulder, and he was suddenly tripped and flung backwards upon the bed. He opened his mouth to shout, and the corner of the sheet was thrust between his teeth. The Invisible Man had him down grimly, but his arms were free, and he struck and tried to kick savagely.

" Listen to reason, will you? " said the Invisible Man, sticking to him in spite of a pounding in the ribs. " By heaven, you'll madden me in a minute!

" Lie still, you fool! " bawled the Invisible Man in Kemp's ear.

Kemp struggled for another moment, and then lay still.

" If you shout, I'll smash your face," said the Invisible Man, relieving his mouth. " I'm an Invisible Man. It is no foolishness and no magic. I am really an Invisible Man. And I want your help. I don't want to hurt you, but if you behave like a frantic rustic I must. Don't you remember me, Kemp? Griffin, of University College."

" Let me get up," said Kemp. " I'll stop where I am. And let me sit quiet for a minute."

He sat up and felt his neck.

" I am Griffin, of University College, and I have made myself invisible. I am just an ordinary man –a man you have known—made invisible."

" Griffin? " said Kemp.

" Griffin," answered the Voice. " A younger student than you were, almost an albino, six feet

high, and broad—with a pink and white face and
red eyes, who won the medal for chemistry."

"I'm confused," said Kemp.   "My brain is
rioting. What has this to do with Griffin?"

"I *am* Griffin."

Kemp thought. "It's horrible," he said. "But
what devilry must happen to make a man invisible?"

"It's no devilry. It's a process, sane and in-
telligible enough——"

"It's really horrible!" said Kemp. "How on
earth——?"

"It's horrible enough. But I'm wounded and in
pain, and tired . . . Great God! Kemp, you are a
man. Take it steady. Give me some food and
drink, and let me sit down here."

Kemp stared at the bandage as it moved across
the room, then saw a basket chair dragged along
the floor and come to rest near the bed. It creaked,
and the seat was depressed a quarter of an inch
or so. He rubbed his eyes and felt his neck
again. "This beats ghosts," he said, and laughed
stupidly.

"That's better. Thank heaven, you're getting
sensible!"

"Or silly," said Kemp, and knuckled his eyes.

"Give me some whisky. I'm near dead."

"I didn't feel so. Where are you? If I get up
shall I run into you? *There!* All right. Whisky.
. . . Here. Where shall I give it you?"

The chair creaked, and Kemp felt the glass drawn
away from him. He let it go by an effort; his
instinct was all against it. It came to rest poised
twenty inches above the front edge of the chair.
He stared at it in infinite perplexity.

"This is—this *must* be—hypnotism. You must have suggested you are invisible."

"Nonsense!" said the Voice.

"It's frantic!"

"Listen to me."

"I demonstrated conclusively this morning," began Kemp, "that invisibility——"

"Never mind what you've demonstrated! I'm starving," said the Voice, "and the night is chilly to a man without clothes."

"Food?" said Kemp.

The tumbler of whisky tilted itself. "Yes," said the Invisible Man, rapping it down. "Have you got a dressing-gown?"

Kemp made some exclamation in an undertone. He walked to a wardrobe, and produced a robe of dingy scarlet. "This do?" he asked. It was taken from him. It hung limp for a moment in mid-air, fluttered weirdly, stood full and decorous buttoning itself, and sat down in his chair.

"Drawers, socks, slippers would be a comfort," said the Unseen curtly. "And food."

"Anything. But this is the insanest thing I was ever in, in my life!"

He turned out his drawers for the articles, and then went downstairs to ransack his larder. He came back with some cold cutlets and bread, pulled up a light table, and placed them before his guest.

"Never mind knives," said his visitor, and a cutlet hung in mid-air with a sound of gnawing.

"I always like to get something about me before I eat," said the Invisible Man, with a full mouth, eating greedily. "Queer fancy."

"I suppose that wrist is all right?" said Kemp.

"Trust me," said the Invisible Man.

"Of all the strange and wonderful——"

"Exactly. But it's odd I should blunder into *your* house to get my bandaging. My first stroke of luck! Anyhow, I meant to sleep in this house to-night. You must stand that! It's a filthy nuisance, my blood showing, isn't it? Quite a clot over there. Gets visible as it coagulates, I see. It's only the living tissue I've changed, and only for as long as I'm alive. . . . I've been in the house three hours."

"But how's it done?" began Kemp, in a tone of exasperation. "Confound it! The whole business— it's unreasonable from beginning to end."

"Quite reasonable," said the Invisible Man; "perfectly reasonable."

He reached over and secured the whisky bottle. Kemp stared at the devouring dressing-gown. A ray of candle-light penetrating a torn patch in the right shoulder made a triangle of light under the left ribs.

"What were the shots?" he asked. "How did the shooting begin?"

"There was a fool of a man—a sort of confederate of mine, curse him!—who tried to steal my money. Has done so."

"Is he invisible, too?"

"No."

"Well?"

"Can't I have some more to eat before I tell all that? I'm hungry—in pain. And you want me to tell stories!"

Kemp got up. "*You* didn't do any shooting?" he asked.

"Not me," said his visitor. "Some fool I'd never

seen fired at random. A lot of them got scared.
They all got scared at me. Curse them! I say—I
want more to eat than this, Kemp."

"I'll see what there is more to eat downstairs,"
said Kemp. "Not much, I'm afraid."

After he had done eating—and he made a heavy
meal—the Invisible Man demanded a cigar. He
bit the end savagely, before Kemp could find a
knife, and cursed when the outer leaf loosened.

It was strange to see him smoking; his mouth and
throat, pharynx and nares, became visible as a sort
of whirling smoke cast.

"This blessed gift of smoking," he said, and
puffed vigorously. "I'm lucky to have fallen upon
you, Kemp. You must help me. Fancy tumbling
on you just now! I'm in a devilish scrape—I've
been mad, I think. The things I have been through!
But we will do things yet, let me tell you."

He helped himself to more whisky and soda.
Kemp got up, looked about him, and fetched
himself a glass from his spare room.

"It's wild—but I suppose I may drink."

"You haven't changed much, Kemp, these dozen
years. You fair men don't. Cool and methodical.
. . . I must tell you. We will work together!"

"But how was it all done?" said Kemp, "and
how did you get like this?"

"For God's sake let me smoke in peace for a
little while, and then I will begin to tell you."

But the story was not told that night. The Invisible
Man's wrist was growing painful; he was feverish,
exhausted, and his mind came round to brood upon
his chase down the hill and the struggle about the
inn. He began his story and fell away from it. He

spoke in fragments of Marvel, he smoked faster, his voice grew angry. Kemp tried to gather what he could.

" He was afraid of me—I could see he was afraid of me," said the Invisible Man many times over. " He meant to give me the slip—he was always casting about! What a fool I was!

" The cur!

" I was furious. I should have killed him——"

" Where did you get the money? " asked Kemp abruptly.

The Invisible Man was silent for a space. " I can't tell you to-night."

He groaned suddenly and leaned forward, supporting his invisible head on invisible hands.

" Kemp," he said, " I've had no sleep for near three days, except a couple of dozes of an hour or so. I must sleep soon."

" Well, have my room—have this room."

" But how can I sleep? If I sleep—he will get away. Ugh! What does it matter? "

" What's the shot wound? " asked Kemp.

" Nothing—scratch and blood. Oh, God! How I want sleep! "

" Why not? "

The Invisible Man appeared to be regarding Kemp. " Because I've a particular objection to being caught by my fellow-men," he said slowly.

Kemp started.

" Fool that I am! " said the Invisible Man, striking the table smartly. " I've put the idea into your head."

18

The Invisible Man Sleeps

EXHAUSTED and wounded as the Invisible Man was, he refused to accept Kemp's word that his freedom should be respected. He examined the two windows of the bedroom, drew up the blinds and opened the sashes to confirm Kemp's statement that a retreat by them would be possible. Outside the night was very quiet and still, and the new moon was setting over the down. Then he examined the keys of the bedroom and the two dressing-room doors, to satisfy himself that these also could be made an assurance of freedom. Finally he expressed himself satisfied. He stood on the hearthrug and Kemp heard the sound of a yawn.

" I'm sorry," said the Invisible Man, " if I cannot tell you all that I have done to-night. But I am worn out. It's grotesque, no doubt. It's horrible! But, believe me, Kemp, in spite of your arguments of this morning, it is quite a possible thing. I have made a discovery. I meant to keep it to myself. I can't. I must have a partner. And you . . . We can do such things . . . But to-morrow. Now, Kemp, I feel as though I must sleep or perish."

Kemp stood in the middle of the room staring at the headless garment. " I suppose I must leave you," he said. " It's—incredible. Three things happening like this, overturning all my preconceptions—would make me insane. But it's real! Is there anything more that I can get you?"

"Only bid me good-night," said Griffin.

"Good-night," said Kemp, and shook an invisible hand. He walked sideways to the door.

Suddenly the dressing-gown walked quickly towards him. "Understand me!" said the dressing-gown. "No attempts to hamper me or capture me! Or——"

Kemp's face changed a little. "I thought I gave you my word," he said.

Kemp closed the door softly behind him, and the key was turned upon him forthwith. Then as he stood with an expression of passive amazement on his face, the rapid feet came to the door of the dressing-room, and that too was locked. Kemp slapped his brow with his hand. "Am I dreaming? Has the world gone mad, or have I?"

He laughed, and put his hand to the locked door. "Barred out of my own bedroom by a flagrant absurdity!" he said.

He walked to the head of the staircase, turned, and stared at the locked doors. "It's fact," he said. He put his fingers to his slightly bruised neck. "Undeniable fact!

"But——" He shook his head hopelessly, turned, and went downstairs.

He lit the dining-room lamp, got out a cigar, and began pacing the room, ejaculating. Now and then he would argue with himself.

"Invisible!" he said.

"Is there such a thing as an invisible animal! . . . In the sea, yes. Thousands—millions. All the larvæ, all the little nauplii and tornarias, all the microscopic things—the jelly-fish! In the sea there are more things invisible than visible! I never thought of that before. . . . And in the ponds too! All those little pond-life things—specks of colourless, translucent jelly! . . . But in air! No!

"It can't be."

"But after all—why not?

"If a man were made of glass he would still be visible."

His meditation became profound. The bulk of three cigars had diffused as a white ash over the carpet before he spoke again. Then it was merely an exclamation. He turned aside, walked out of the room, went into his little consulting-room and lit the gas there. It was a little room, because Dr. Kemp did not live by practice, and in it were the day's newspapers. The morning's paper lay carelessly opened and thrown aside. He caught it up, turned it over, and read the account of a "Strange Story from Iping" that the mariner at Port Stowe had spelt over so painfully to Marvel. Kemp read it swiftly.

"Wrapped up!" said Kemp. "Disguised! Hiding it! 'No one seems to have been aware of his misfortune.' What the devil *is* his game?"

He dropped the paper and his eye went seeking. "Ah!" he said, and caught up the *St. James's Gazette*, lying folded up as it arrived. "Now we shall get at the truth," said Dr. Kemp. He rent the paper open. A couple of columns confronted him. "An Entire Village in Sussex goes Mad," was the heading.

"Good Heavens!" said Kemp, reading eagerly an incredulous account of the events in Iping of the previous afternoon, that have already been described. Over the leaf the report in the morning paper had been re-printed.

He re-read it. " Ran through the streets striking right and left. Jaffers insensible. Mr. Huxter in great pain—still unable to describe what he saw. Painful humiliation—vicar. Woman ill with terror. Windows smashed. This extraordinary story probably a fabrication. Too good not to print— *cum grano*."

He dropped the paper and stared blankly in front of him. " Probably a fabrication! "

He caught up the paper again, and re-read the whole business.

" But when does the Tramp come in? Why the deuce was he chasing a tramp? "

He sat down abruptly on the surgical couch.

" He's not only invisible," he said, " but he's mad! Homicidal! . . ."

When dawn came to mingle its pallor with the lamplight and cigar-smoke of the dining-room, Kemp was still pacing up and down, trying to grasp the incredible.

He was altogether too excited to sleep. His servants, descending sleepily, discovered him, and were inclined to think that over-study had worked this ill on him. He gave them extraordinary but quite explicit instructions to lay breakfast for two in the belvedere study, and then to confine themselves to the basement and ground floor. Then he continued to pace the dining-room until the morning's paper came. That had much to say and little to tell, beyond the confirmation of the evening before, and a very badly written account of another remarkable tale from Port Burdock. This gave Kemp the essence of the happenings at the " Jolly Cricketers," and the name of Marvel. " He has made me keep with him twenty-four hours," Marvel testified. Certain minor facts were added to the Iping story, notably the cutting of the village telegraph wire. But there was nothing to throw light on the connection between the Invisible Man and the tramp—for Mr. Marvel had supplied no information about the three books or the money with which he was lined. The incredulous tone had vanished, and a shoal of reporters and inquirers were already at work elaborating the matter.

Kemp read every scrap of the report, and sent his housemaid out to get every one of the morning papers she could. These also he devoured.

" He is invisible! " he said. " And it reads like rage growing to mania! The things he may do! The things he may do! And he's upstairs free as the air. What on earth ought I to do?

" For instance, would it be a breach of faith if—— No."

He went to a little untidy desk in the corner, and began a note. He tore this up half written, and wrote another. He read it over and considered it. Then he took an envelope and addressed it to " Colonel Adye, Port Burdock."

The Invisible Man awoke even as Kemp was doing this. He awoke in an evil temper, and Kemp, alert for every sound, heard his pattering feet rush suddenly across the bedroom overhead. Then a chair was flung over and the washhand-stand tumbler smashed. Kemp hurried upstairs and tapped eagerly.

19

Certain First Principles

" WHAT'S the matter? " asked Kemp, when the Invisible Man admitted him.

" Nothing," was the answer.

" But, confound it! The smash? "

" Fit of temper," said the Invisible Man. " Forgot this arm; and it's sore."

" You're rather liable to that sort of thing."

" I am."

Kemp walked across the room and picked up the fragments of broken glass. " All the facts are out about you," said Kemp, standing up with the glass in his hand. " All that happened in Iping and down the hill. The world has become aware of its invisible citizen. But no one knows you are here."

The Invisible Man swore.

" The secret's out. I gather it was a secret. I don't know what your plans are, but, of course, I'm anxious to help you."

The Invisible Man sat down on the bed.

" There's breakfast upstairs," said Kemp, speaking as easily as possible, and he was delighted to find his strange guest rose willingly. Kemp led the way up the narrow staircase to the belvedere.

" Before we can do anything else," said Kemp, " I must understand a little more about this invisibility of yours." He had sat down, after one

nervous glance out of the window, with the air of
a man who has talking to do. His doubts of the
sanity of the entire business flashed and vanished
again as he looked across to where Griffin sat at the
breakfast-table, a headless, handless dressing-gown,
wiping unseen lips on a miraculously held serviette.

"It's simple enough—and credible enough," said
Griffin, putting the serviette aside.

"No doubt to you, but——" Kemp laughed.

"Well, yes, to me it seemed wonderful at first,
no doubt. But now, Great God! . . . But we will
do great things yet! I came on the stuff first at
Chesilstowe."

"Chesilstowe?"

"I went there after I left London. You know
I dropped medicine and took up physics? No; well,
I did. *Light* fascinated me."

"Ah!"

"Optical density! The whole subject is a network
of riddles—a network with solutions glimmering
elusively through. And being but two-and-twenty
and full of enthusiasm, I said: 'I will devote my
life to this. This is worth while.' You know what
fools we are at two-and-twenty?"

"Fools then or fools now," said Kemp.

"As though knowing could be any satisfaction
to a man!

"But I went to work—like a nigger. And I had
hardly worked and thought about the matter six
months before light came through one of the meshes
suddenly—blindingly! I found a general principle
of pigments and refraction—a formula, a geometrical
expression involving four dimensions. Fools, common men—even common mathematicians, do not

know anything of what some general expression may mean to the student of molecular physics. In the books—the books that tramp has hidden—there are marvels, miracles! But this was not a method, it was an idea that might lead to a method by which it would be possible without changing any other property of matter—except in some instances colours—to lower the refractive index of a substance, solid or liquid, to that of air, so far as all practical purposes are concerned."

" Phew! " said Kemp. " That's odd! But still I don't see quite . . . I can understand that thereby you could spoil a valuable stone, but personal invisibility is a far cry."

" Precisely," said Griffin. " But consider, visibility depends on the action of the visible bodies on light. Let me put the elementary facts to you as if you did not know. It will make my meaning clearer. You know quite well that either a body absorbs light or it reflects or refracts it or does all these things. If it neither reflects nor refracts nor absorbs light, it cannot of itself be visible. You see an opaque red box, for instance, because the colour absorbs some of the light and reflects the rest, all the red part of the light to you. If it did not absorb any particular part of the light, but reflected it all, then it would be a shining white box. Silver! A diamond box would neither absorb much of the light nor reflect much from the general surface, but just here and there where the surfaces are favourable the light would be reflected and refracted, so that you would get a brilliant appearance of flashing reflections and translucencies. A sort of skeleton of light. A glass box would not be so brilliant, not so clearly visible as a diamond box, because there would be less refraction and reflection. See that? From certain points of view you would see quite clearly through it. Some kinds of glass would be more visible than others—a box of flint glass would be brighter than a box of ordinary window glass. A box of very thin, common glass would be hard to see in a bad light, because it would absorb hardly any light and refract and reflect very little. And if you put a sheet of common white glass in water, still more if you put it in some denser liquid than water, it would vanish almost altogether, because light passing from water to glass is only slightly refracted or reflected, or, indeed, affected in any way. It is almost as invisible as a jet of coal gas or hydrogen is in air. And for precisely the same reason!"

"Yes," said Kemp, "that is plain sailing. Any schoolboy nowadays knows all that."

"And here is another fact any schoolboy will know. If a sheet of glass is smashed, Kemp, and beaten into a powder, it becomes much more visible while it is in the air; it becomes at last an opaque, white powder. This is because the powdering multiplies the surfaces of the glass at which refraction and reflection occur. In the sheet of glass there are only two surfaces, in the powder the light is reflected or refracted by each grain it passes through, and very little gets right through the powder. But if the white, powdered glass is put into water it forthwith vanishes. The powdered glass and water have much the same refractive index, that is, the light undergoes very little refraction or reflection in passing from one to the other.

"You make the glass invisible by putting it into a liquid of nearly the same refractive index, a transparent thing becomes invisible if it is put in any medium of almost the same refractive index. And if you will consider only a second, you will see also that the powder of glass might be made to vanish in air, if its refractive index could be made the same as that of air. For then there would be no refraction or reflection as the light passed from glass to air."

"Yes, yes," said Kemp. "But a man's not powdered glass!"

"No," said Griffin. "*He's more transparent!*"

"Nonsense!"

"That's from a doctor! How one forgets! Have you already forgotten your physics in ten years? Just think of all the things that are transparent and seem not to be so! Paper, for instance, is made up of transparent fibres, and it is white and opaque only for the same reason that a powder or glass is white and opaque. Oil white paper, fill up the interstices between the particles with oil, so that there is no longer refraction or reflection except at the surfaces, and it becomes as transparent as glass. And not only paper, but cotton fibre, linen fibre, wool fibre, woody fibre, and *bone*, Kemp, *flesh*, Kemp, *hair*, Kemp, *nails* and *nerves*, Kemp; in fact, the whole fabric of a man, except the red of his blood and the dark pigment of hair, are all made up of transparent, colourless tissue—so little suffices to make us visible one to the other. For the most part, the fibres of a living creature are no more opaque than water."

"Of course, of course!" cried Kemp. "I was

thinking only last night of the sea larvæ and jelly-fish!"

"*Now* you have me! And all that I knew and had in mind a year after I left London—six years ago. But I kept it to myself. I had to do my work under frightful disadvantages. Hobbema, my professor, was a scientific bounder, a thief of ideas—he was always prying! And you know the knavish system of the scientific world. I simply would not publish and let him share my credit. I went on working; I got nearer and nearer making my formula into an experiment—a reality. I told no living soul, because I meant to flash my work upon the world with crushing effect and become famous at a blow. I took up the question of pigments to fill up certain gaps, and suddenly—not by design, but by accident—I made a discovery in physiology."

"Yes?"

"You know the red colouring matter of blood—it can be made white—colourless—and remain with all the functions it has now!"

Kemp gave a cry of incredulous amazement.

The Invisible Man rose and began pacing the little study. "You may well exclaim. I remember that night. It was late at night—in the daytime one was bothered with the gaping, silly students—and I worked there sometimes till dawn. It came suddenly, splendid and complete, into my mind. I was alone, the laboratory was still, with the tall lights burning brightly and silently. . . . 'One could make an animal—a tissue—transparent! One could make it invisible! All except the pigments. I could be Invisible,' I said, suddenly realising what it meant to be an albino with such knowledge. It was overwhelming. I left the filtering I was doing, and went and stared out of the great window at the stars. ' I could be Invisible,' I repeated.

" To do such a thing would be to transcend magic. And I beheld, unclouded by doubt, a magnificent vision of all that Invisibility might mean to a man. The mystery, the power, the freedom. Drawbacks I saw none. You have only to think! And I, a shabby, poverty-struck, hemmed in demonstrator, teaching fools in a provincial college, might suddenly become—this. I ask you, Kemp, if *you*. . . . Anyone, I tell you, would have flung himself upon that research. And I worked three years, and every mountain of difficulty I toiled over showed another from its summit. The infinite details! And the exasperation! A professor, a provincial professor, always prying. ' When are you going to publish this work of yours? ' was his everlasting question. And the students, the cramped means! Three years I had of it——

" And after three years of secrecy and trouble, I found that to complete it was impossible— impossible."

" How? " asked Kemp.

" Money," said the Invisible Man, and went again to stare out of the window.

He turned round abruptly. " I robbed the old man—robbed my father.

" The money was not his, and he shot himself."

20

At the House in Great Portland Street

FOR a moment Kemp sat in silence, staring at the back of the headless figure at the window. Then he started, struck by a thought, rose, took the Invisible Man's arm, and turned him away from the outlook.

" You are tired," he said, " and while I sit you walk about. Have my chair."

He placed himself between Griffin and the nearest window.

For a space Griffin sat silent, and then he resumed abruptly:

" I had left the Chesilstowe College already," he said, " when that happened. It was last December. I had taken a room in London, a large unfurnished room in a big, ill-managed lodging-house in a slum near Great Portland Street. The room was soon full of the appliances I had bought with his money, and the work was going on steadily, successfully, drawing near an end. I was like a man emerging from a thicket, and suddenly coming on some un-meaning tragedy. I went to bury my father. My mind was still on this research, and I did not lift a finger to save his character. I remember the funeral, the cheap hearse, the scant ceremony, the windy, frost-bitten hillside, and the old college friend of his who read the service over him—a shabby, black, bent old man with a snivelling cold.

" I remember walking back to the empty home through the place that had once been a village and was now patched and tinkered by the jerry builders into the ugly likeness of a town. Every way the roads ran out at last into the desecrated fields and ended in rubble heaps and rank, wet weeds. I remember myself as a gaunt, black figure, going along the slippery, shiny side-walk, and the strange sense of detachment I felt from the squalid respectability, the sordid commercialism of the place. . . .

" I did not feel a bit sorry for my father. He seemed to me to be the victim of his own foolish sentimentality. The current cant required my attendance at his funeral, but it was really not my affair.

" But going along the High Street my old life came back to me for a space. I met the girl I had known ten years since. Our eyes met. . . .

" Something moved me to turn back and talk to her. She was a very ordinary person.

" It was all like a dream, that visit to the old place. I did not feel then that I was lonely, that I had come out from the world into a desolation. I appreciated my loss of sympathy, but I put it down to the general inanity of life. Re-entering my room seemed like the recovery of reality. There were the things I knew and loved. There stood the apparatus, the experiments arranged and waiting. And now there was scarcely a difficulty left, beyond the planning of details.

" I will tell you, Kemp, sooner or later, all the complicated processes. We need not go into that now. For the most part, saving certain gaps I chose to remember, they are written in cipher in those books that tramp has hidden. We must hunt him down. We must get those books again. But the essential phase was to place the transparent object whose refractive index was to be lowered, between two radiating centres of a sort of ethereal vibration, of which I will tell you more fully later. No—not these Röntgen vibrations; I don't know that these others of mine have been described, yet they are obvious enough. I needed two little dynamos— principally, and these I worked with a cheap gas-engine. . . . My first experiment was with a bit of white wool fabric. It was the strangest thing in the world to see it soft and white in the flicker of the flashes, and then to watch it fade like a wreath of smoke and vanish.

" I could scarcely believe I had done it. I put my hand into the emptiness and there was the thing as solid as ever. I felt it awkwardly, and threw it on the floor. I had a little trouble finding it again.

" And then came a curious experience. I heard a miaow behind me, and, turning, saw a lean white cat, very dirty, on the cistern cover outside the window. A thought came into my head. ' Everything ready for you,' I said, and went to the window, opened it, and called softly. She came in, purring —the poor beast was starving—and I gave her some milk. All my food was in a cupboard in the corner of the room. After that she went smelling round the room, evidently with the idea of making herself at home. The invisible rag upset her a bit; you should have seen her spit at it! But I made her comfortable on the pillow of my truckle-bed, and I gave her butter to get her to wash."

" And you processed her? "

" I processed her. But giving drugs to a cat is no joke, Kemp! And the process failed."

" Failed? "

" In two particulars. These were the claws and the pigment stuff—what is it? At the back of the eye in a cat. You know? "

" *Tapetum.*"

" Yes, the *tapetum.* It didn't go. After I'd given the stuff to bleach the blood and done certain other things to her, I gave the beast opium, and put her and the pillow she was sleeping on, on the apparatus. And after all the rest had faded and vanished, there remained the two little ghosts of her eyes."

" Odd."

" I can't explain it. She was bandaged and clamped of course—so I had her safe, but she awoke while she was still misty, and miawled dismally, and someone came knocking. It was an old woman from downstairs, who suspected me of vivisecting—a drink-sodden old creature, with only a cat to care for in all the world. I whipped out some chloroform, applied it, and answered the door. ' Did I hear a cat? ' she asked. ' My cat? ' ' Not here,' said I, very politely. She was a little doubtful, and tried to peer past me into the room—strange enough to her, no doubt, bare walls, uncurtained windows, truckle-bed, with the gas-engine vibrating, and the seethe of the radiant points, and that faint stinging of chloroform in the air. She had to be satisfied at last, and went away again."

" How long did it take? " asked Kemp.

" Three or four hours—the cat. The bones and sinews and the fat were the last to go, and the tips of the coloured hairs. And, as I say, the back part of the eye, tough, iridescent stuff it is, wouldn't go at all.

" It was night outside long before the business was over, and nothing was to be seen but the dim eyes and the claws. I stopped the gas-engine, felt for and stroked the beast, which was still insensible, released its fastenings, and then, being tired, left it sleeping on the invisible pillow and went to bed. I found it hard to sleep. I lay awake thinking weak, aimless stuff, going over the experiment again and again, or dreaming feverishly of things growing misty and vanishing about me until everything, the ground I stood on, vanished, and so I came to that sickly, falling nightmare one gets. About two the cat began miawling about the room. I tried to hush it by talking to it, and then I decided to turn it out. I remember the shock I had striking a light— there were just the round eyes shining green—and nothing round them. I would have given it milk, but I hadn't any. It wouldn't be quiet, it just sat down and miaowed at the door. I tried to catch it, with an idea of putting it out of the window, but it wouldn't be caught, it vanished. It kept on miaowing in different parts of the room. At last I opened the window and made a bustle. I suppose it went out at last. I never saw nor heard any more of it. Then—Heaven knows why—I fell thinking of my father's funeral again, and the dismal, windy hillside, until the day had come. I found sleep was hopeless, and, locking my door after me, wandered out into the morning streets."

" You don't mean to say there's an Invisible Cat at large in the world? " said Kemp.

"If it hasn't been killed," said the Invisible Man. "Why not?"

"Why not?" said Kemp. "I didn't mean to interrupt."

"It's very probably been killed," said the Invisible Man. "It was alive four days after, I know, and down a grating in Great Tichfield Street, because I saw a crowd round the place trying to see whence the miaowing came."

He was silent for the best part of a minute. Then he resumed abruptly: "I remember that morning before the change very vividly.

"I must have gone up Great Portland Street— for I remember the barracks in Albany Street and the horse soldiers coming out, and at last I found myself sitting in the sunshine and feeling very ill and strange on the summit of Primrose Hill. It was a sunny day in January—one of those sunny, frosty days that came before the snow this year. My weary brain tried to formulate the position, to plot out a plan of action.

"I was surprised to find, now that my prize was within my grasp, how inconclusive its attainment seemed. As a matter of fact I was worked out, the intense stress of nearly four years' continuous work left me incapable of any strength or feeling. I was apathetic, and I tried in vain to recover the enthusiasm of my first inquiries, the passion of discovery that had enabled me to compass even the downfall of my father's grey hairs. Nothing seemed to matter. I saw pretty clearly this was a transient mood, due to overwork and want of sleep, and that either by drugs or rest it would be possible to recover my energies.

"All I could think clearly was that the thing had to be carried through; the fixed idea still ruled me. And soon, for the money I had was almost exhausted. I looked about me at the hillside with children playing and girls watching them, and tried to think of all the fantastic advantages an invisible man would have in the world. After a time I crawled home, took some food and a strong dose of strychnine, and went to sleep in my clothes on my unmade bed. . . . Strychnine is a grand tonic, Kemp, to take the flabbiness out of a man."

"It's the devil," said Kemp. "It's the palæolithic in a bottle."

"I awoke vastly invigorated and rather irritable. You know?"

"I know the stuff."

"And there was someone rapping at the door. It was my landlord with threats and inquiries, an old Polish Jew in a long grey coat and greasy slippers. I had been tormenting a cat in the night, he was sure—the old woman's tongue had been busy. He insisted on knowing all about it. The laws of this country against vivisection were very severe—he might be liable. I denied the cat. Then the vibration of the little gas-engine could be felt all over the house, he said. That was true, certainly. He edged round me into the room, peering about over his German silver spectacles, and a sudden dread came into my mind that he might carry away something of my secret. I tried to keep between him and the concentrating apparatus I had arranged, and that only made him more curious. What was I doing? Why was I always alone and secretive? Was it legal? Was it dangerous? I paid nothing but the usual rent. His had always been a most respectable house—in a disreputable neighbourhood. Suddenly my temper gave way. I told him to get out. He began to protest, to jabber of his right of entry. In a moment I had him by the collar—something ripped—and he went spinning out into his own passage. I slammed and locked the door and sat down quivering.

" He made a fuss outside, which I disregarded, and after a time he went away.

" But this brought matters to a crisis. I did not know what he would do, nor even what he had the power to do. To move to fresh apartments would have meant delay—altogether I had barely twenty pounds left in the world, for the most part in a bank —and I could not afford that. Vanish! It was irresistible. Then there would be an inquiry, the sacking of my room.

" At the thought of the possibility of my work being exposed or interrupted at its very climax, I became angry and active. I hurried out with my three books of notes, my cheque book—the tramp has them now—and directed them from the nearest Post Office to a house of call for letters and parcels in Great Portland Street. I tried to go out noiselessly. Coming in, I found my landlord going quietly upstairs—he had heard the door close, I suppose. You would have laughed to see him jump aside on the landing as I came tearing after him. He glared at me as I went by him, and I made the house quiver with the slamming of my door. I heard him come shuffling up to my door, hesitate, and go down. I set to work upon my preparations forthwith.

"It was all done that evening and night. While I was still sitting under the sickly, drowsy influence of the drugs that decolourise blood, there came a repeated knocking at the door. It ceased, footsteps went away and returned, and the knocking was resumed. There was an attempt to push something under the door—a blue paper. Then in a fit of irritation I rose, and went and flung the door wide open. 'Now then?' said I.

"It was the landlord, with a notice of ejectment or something. He held it out to me, saw something odd about my hands, I expect, and lifted his eyes to my face.

"For a moment he gaped. Then he gave a sort of inarticulate cry, dropped candle and writ together, and went blundering down the dark passage to the stairs.

"I shut the door, locked it, and went to the looking-glass. Then I understood his terror. . . . My face was white—like white stone.

"But it was all horrible. I had not expected the suffering. A night of racking anguish, sickness, and fainting. I set my teeth, though my skin was presently afire, all my body afire, but I lay there like grim death. I understood now how it was the cat had howled until I chloroformed it. Lucky it was I lived alone and untended in my room. There were times when I sobbed, and groaned, and talked. But I stuck to it. . . . I became insensible, and woke languid in the darkness.

"The pain had passed. I thought I was killing myself, and I did not care. I shall never forget that dawn, and the strange horror of seeing that my hands had become as clouded glass, and watching them grow clearer and thinner as the day went by, until at last I could see the sickly disorder of my room through them, though I closed my transparent eyelids. My limbs became glassy, the bones and arteries faded, vanished, and the little white nerves went last. I gritted my teeth and stayed there to the end. . . . At last only the dead tips of the finger-nails remained, pallid and white, and the brown stain of some acid upon my fingers.

" I struggled up. At first I was as incapable as a swathed infant—stepping with limbs I could not see. I was weak and very hungry. I went and stared at nothing in my shaving-glass—at nothing, save where an attentuated pigment still remained behind the retina of my eyes, fainter than mist. I had to hang on to the table and press my forehead to the glass.

" It was only by a frantic effort of will that I dragged myself back to the apparatus, and completed the process.

" I slept during the forenoon, pulling a sheet over my eyes to shut out the light, and about midday I was awakened again by a knocking. My strength had returned. I sat up and listened and heard a whispering. I sprang to my feet, and as noiselessly as possible began to detach the connections of my apparatus, and to distribute it about the room so as to destroy the suggestions of its arrangement. Presently the knocking was renewed and voices called, first my landlord's and then two others. To gain time I answered them. The invisible rag and pillow came to hand, and I opened the window and pitched them out on to the cistern cover. As the window opened a heavy crash came at the door.

Someone had charged it with the idea of smashing the lock. But the stout bolts I had screwed up some days before stopped him. That startled me—made me angry. I began to tremble and do things hurriedly.

" I tossed together some loose paper, straw, packing-paper, and so forth, in the middle of the room, and turned on the gas. Heavy blows began to rain upon the door. I could not find the matches. I beat my hands on the wall with rage. I turned down the gas again, stepped out of the window on the cistern cover, very softly lowered the sash, and sat down, secure and invisible, but quivering with anger, to watch events. They split a panel, I saw, and in another moment they had broken away the staples of the bolts and stood in the open doorway. It was the landlord and his two step-sons—sturdy young men of three or four-and-twenty. Behind them fluttered the old hag of a woman from downstairs.

" You may imagine their astonishment at finding the room empty. One of the younger men rushed to the window at once, flung it open and stared out. His staring eyes, and thick-lipped, bearded face came a foot from my face. I was half-minded to hit his silly countenance, but I arrested my doubled fist.

" He stared right through me. So did the others as they joined him. The old man went and peered under the bed, and then they all made a rush for the cupboard. They had to argue about it at length in Yiddish and Cockney English. They concluded I had not answered them, that their imagination had deceived them. A feeling of extraordinary

elation took the place of my anger as I sat outside
the window and watched these four people—for the
old lady came in, glancing suspiciously about her
like a cat—trying to understand the riddle of my
existence.

" The old man, so far as I could understand his
polyglot, agreed with the old lady that I was a
vivisectionist. The sons protested in garbled English
that I was an electrician, and appealed to the
dynamos and radiators. They were all nervous
against my arrival, although I found subsequently
that they had bolted the front door. The old lady
peered into the cupboard and under the bed. One
of my fellow-lodgers, a costermonger, who shared
the opposite room with a butcher, appeared on the
landing, and he was called in, and told incoherent
things.

" It occurred to me that the peculiar radiators I
had, if they fell into the hands of some acute, well-
educated person, would give me away too much,
and, watching my opportunity, I descended from
the window-sill into the room and dodging the old
woman tilted one of the little dynamos off its fellow
on which it was standing, and smashed both
apparatus. How scared they were! . . . Then, while
they were trying to explain the smash, I slipped out
of the room and went softly downstairs.

" I went into one of the sitting-rooms and waited
until they came down, still speculative and argumentative, all a little disappointed at finding no
' horrors,' and all a little puzzled how they stood
legally towards me. As soon as they had gone on
down to the basement, I slipped up again with a
box of matches, fired my heap of paper and rubbish,

put the chairs and bedding thereby, led the gas to the affair by means of an indiarubber tube——"

"You fired the house?" exclaimed Kemp.

"Fired the house! It was the only way to cover my trail, and no doubt it was insured. . . . I slipped the bolts of the front door quietly and went out into the street. I was invisible, and I was only just beginning to realise the extraordinary advantage my invisibility gave me. My head was already teeming with plans of all the wild and wonderful things I had now impunity to do.

21

In Oxford Street

" IN going downstairs the first time I found an un-expected difficulty because I could not see my feet; indeed, I stumbled twice, and there was an unaccustomed clumsiness in gripping the bolt. By not looking down, however, I managed to walk on the level passably well.

" My mood, I say, was one of exaltation. I felt as a seeing man might do, with padded feet and noiseless clothes, in a city of the blind. I experienced a wild impulse to jest, to startle people, to clap them on the back, fling people's hats astray, and generally revel in my extraordinary advantage.

" But hardly had I emerged upon Great Portland Street, however (my lodging was close to the big draper's shop there) when I heard a clashing concussion, and was hit violently behind, and turning, saw a man carrying a basket of soda-water siphons, and looking in amazement at his burden. Although the blow had really hurt me, I found something so irresistible in his astonishment that I laughed aloud. 'The devil's in the basket,' I said, and suddenly twisted it out of his hand. He left go incontinently, and I swung the whole weight up into the air.

" But a fool of a cabman, standing outside a public-house, made a sudden rush for this, and his extended fingers took me with excruciating violence under the ear. I let the whole down with a smash

on the cabman, and then, with shouts and the clatter
of feet about me, people coming out of shops,
vehicles pulling up, I realised what I had done for
myself, and cursing my folly, backed against a shop
window and prepared to dodge out of the confusion.
In a moment I should be wedged into a crowd and
inevitably discovered. I pushed by a butcher boy,
who luckily did not turn to see the nothingness that
shoved him aside, and dodged behind the cabman's
four-wheeler. I do not know how they settled the
business. I hurried straight across the road, which
was happily clear, and hardly heeding which way
I went in the fright of detection the incident had
given me, plunged into the afternoon throng of
Oxford Street.

" I tried to get into the stream of people, but they
were too thick for me, and in a moment my heels
were being trodden upon. I took the gutter, the
roughness of which I found painful to my feet, and
forthwith the shaft of a crawling hansom dug me
forcibly under the shoulder blade, reminding me
that I was already bruised severely. I staggered
out of the way of the cab, avoided a perambulator
by a convulsive movement, and found myself behind
the hansom. A happy thought saved me, and as
this drove slowly along I followed on its immediate
wake, trembling and astonished at the turn of my
adventure, and not only trembling but shivering.
It was a bright day in January, and I was stark
naked, and the thin slime of mud that covered the
road was near freezing. Foolish as it seems to me
now, I had not reckoned that, transparent or not,
I was still amenable to the weather and all its
consequences.

" Then suddenly a bright idea came into my head. I ran round and got into the cab. And so, shivering, scared, and sniffing with the first intimations of a cold, and with the bruises in the small of my back growing upon my attention, I drove slowly along Oxford Street and past Tottenham Court Road. My mood was as different from that in which I had sallied forth ten minutes since as it is possible to imagine. *This* invisibility, indeed! The one thought that possessed me now was how to get out of the scrape I was in?

" We crawled past Mudie's, and there a tall woman, with five or six yellow-labelled books, hailed my cab, and I sprang out just in time to escape her, shaving a railway van narrowly in my flight. I made off up the roadway to Bloomsbury Square, intending to strike north beyond the Museum, and so get into the quiet district. I was now cruelly chilled, and the strangeness of my situation so unnerved me that I whimpered as I ran. At the westward corner of the square a little white dog ran out of the Pharmaceutical Society's offices, and incontinently made for me, nose down.

" I had never realised it before, but the nose is to the mind of a dog what the eye is to the mind of a seeing man. Dogs perceive the scent of a man moving as men perceive his visible appearance. This brute began barking and leaping, showing, as it seemed to me only too plainly, that he was aware of me. I crossed Great Russell Street, glancing over my shoulder as I did so, and went some way along Montague Street before I realised what I was running towards.

" Then I became aware of a blare of music, and

looking along the street saw a number of people advancing out of Russell Square, red jerseys and the banner of the Salvation Army to the fore. Such a crowd, chanting in the roadway and scoffing on the pavement, I could not hope to penetrate, and dreading to go back and farther from home again, and, deciding on the spur of the moment, I ran up the white steps of a house facing the Museum railings, and stood there until the crowd should have passed. Happily the dog stopped at the noise of the band, hesitated, and turned tail, running back to Blooms-bury Square again.

"On came the band, bawling with unconscious irony some hymn about 'When shall we see His face?' and it seemed an interminable time to me before the tide of the crowd washed along the pavement by me. Thud, thud, thud, came the drum with a vibrating resonance, and for the moment I did not notice two urchins stopping at the railings by me. "See 'em,' said one. 'See what?' said the other. 'Why—them footmarks—bare. Like what you makes in mud.'

"I looked down and saw the youngsters had stopped and were gaping at the muddy footmarks I had left behind me, up the newly whitened steps. The passing people elbowed and jostled them, but their confounded intelligence was arrested. 'Thud, thud, thud, when, thud, shall we see, thud, His face, thud, thud.' 'There's a barefoot man gone up them steps, or I don't know nothing,' said one. 'And he ain't never come down again. And his foot was a-bleeding.'

"The thick of the crowd had already passed. 'Looky there, Ted,' quoth the younger of the detectives with the sharpness of surprise in his voice, and pointed straight at my feet. I looked down and saw at once the dim suggestion of their outline sketched in splashes of mud. For a moment I was paralysed.

" ' Why, that's rum! ' said the elder. ' Dashed rum! It's just like the ghost of a foot, ain't it? ' He hesitated and advanced with outstretched hand. A man pulled up short to see what he was catching, and then a girl. In another moment he would have touched me. Then I saw what to do. I made a step, the boy started back with an exclamation, and with a rapid movement I swung myself over into the portico of the next house. But the smaller boy was sharp enough to follow the movement, and before I was well down the steps and upon the pavement he had recovered from his momentary astonishment, and was shouting out that the feet had gone over the wall.

" They rushed round and saw my new footmarks flash into being on the lower step and upon the pavement.

" ' What's up? ' asked someone.

" ' Feet! Look! Feet running! '

" Everybody in the road, except my three pursuers, was pouring along after the Salvation Army, and this flow not only impeded me but them. There was an eddy of surprise and interrogation. At the cost of bowling over one young fellow I got through, and in another moment I was running headlong round the circuit of Russell Square, with six or seven astonished people following my footmarks. There was no time for explanation, or else the whole host would have been after me.

"Twice I doubled round corners, thrice I crossed the road and came back on my tracks, and then as my feet grew hot and dry the damp impressions began to fade. At last I had a breathing space, and rubbed my feet clean with my hands, and so got away altogether. The last I saw of the chase was a little group of a dozen people, perhaps, studying with infinite perplexity a slowly drying footprint that had resulted from a puddle in Tavistock Square, a footprint as isolated and incomprehensible to them as Crusoe's solitary discovery.

"This running warmed me to a certain extent, and I went on with a better courage through the maze of less frequented roads that runs thereabout. My back had now become very stiff and sore, my tonsils were painful from the cabman's fingers, and the skin of my neck had been scratched by his nails; my feet hurt exceedingly, and I was lame from a little cut on one foot. I saw in time a blind man approaching me, and fled limping, for I feared his subtle intuitions. Once or twice accidental collisions occurred, and I left people amazed with unaccountable curses ringing in their ears. Then came something silent and quiet upon my face, and across the square fell a thin veil of slowly falling flakes of snow. I had caught a cold, and do as I would I could not avoid an occasional sneeze. And every dog that came in sight, with its pointing nose and curious sniffing, was a terror to me.

"Then came men and boys running, first one then others, and shouting as they ran. It was a fire. They ran in the direction of my lodging, and looking back down a street I saw a mass of black smoke streaming up above the roofs and telephone wires. It was, I felt assured, my lodging that was burning; my clothes, apparatus, all my resources, indeed, except my cheque-book and the three volumes of memoranda that awaited me in Great Portland Street, were there. Burning! I had burnt my boats—if ever a man did! The place was blazing."

The Invisible Man paused and thought. Kemp glanced nervously out of the window. "Yes!" he said, "go on."

22

In the Emporium

" So last January, with the beginning of a snow-storm in the air about me—and if it settled on me it would betray me!—weary, cold, painful, inexpressibly wretched, and still but half convinced of my invisible quality, I began this new life to which I am committed. I had no refuge, no appliances, no human being in the whole world in whom I could confide. To have told my secret would have given me away—made a mere show and rarity of me. Nevertheless I was half-minded to accost some passer-by and throw myself upon his mercy. But I knew too clearly the terror and brutal cruelty my advances would evoke. I made no plans in the street. My sole object was to get shelter from the snow, to get myself covered and warm, then I might hope to plan. But even to me, an Invisible Man, the rows of London houses stood latched, barred, and bolted impregnably.

" Only one thing could I see clearly before me— the cold, exposure and misery of the snowstorm and night.

" And then I had a brilliant idea. I turned down one of the roads leading from Gower Street to Tottenham Court Road, and found myself outside Omnium's, the big establishment where everything is to be bought—you know the place: meat, grocery, linen, furniture, clothing, oil paintings even —a huge, meandering collection of shops rather than a shop. I had thought I should find the doors open, but they were closed, and as I stood in the wide entrance a carriage stopped outside, and a man in uniform—you know the kind of personage with ' Omnium ' on his cap—flung open the door. I contrived to enter, and walking down the shop— it was a department where they were selling ribbons and gloves and stockings and that sort of thing— came to a more spacious region, devoted to picnic baskets and wicker furniture.

" I did not feel safe there, however, people were going to and fro, and I prowled restlessly about until I came upon a huge section in an upper floor containing multitudes of bedsteads, and over these I clambered, and found a resting-place at last among a huge pile of folded flock mattresses. The place was already lit up and agreeably warm, and I decided to remain in hiding where I was, keeping a cautious eye on the two or three sets of shopmen and customers who were meandering through the place, until closing time came. Then I should be able, I thought, to rob the place for food and clothing and disguise, prowl through it, and examine its resources, perhaps sleep on some of the bedding. That seemed an acceptable plan. My idea was to procure clothing to make myself a muffled but acceptable figure, to get money, and then to recover my books and parcels, where they awaited me, take a lodging somewhere, and elaborate plans for the complete realisation of the advantages my invisibility gave me (as I still imagined) over my fellow-men.

" Closing time arrived quickly enough. It could

not have been more than an hour after I took up my position on the mattresses before I noticed the blinds of the windows being drawn, and customers being marched doorward. And then a number of brisk young men began with remarkable alacrity to tidy up the goods that remained disturbed. I left my lair as the crowds diminished and prowled cautiously out into the less desolate parts of the shop. I was really surprised to observe how rapidly the young men and women whipped away the goods displayed for sale during the day. All the boxes of goods, the hanging fabrics, the festoons of lace, the boxes of sweets in the grocery section, the displays of this and that, were being taken down, folded up, slapped into tidy receptacles, and everything that could not be taken down and put away had sheets of some coarse stuff like sacking flung over it. Finally all the chairs were turned up on the counters, leaving the floors clear. Directly each of these young people had done, he or she made promptly for the door with such an expression of animation as I have rarely observed in a shop-assistant before. Then came a lot of youngsters, scattering sawdust and carrying pails and brooms. I had to dodge to get out of the way, and as it was my ankle got stung with the sawdust. For some time, wandering through the swathed and darkened departments, I could hear the brooms at work. And at last, a good hour or more after the shop had been closed, came a noise of locking doors. Silence came upon the place, and I found myself wandering through the vast and intricate shops, galleries, and showrooms of the place alone. It was very still—in one place I remember passing near one of the Tottenham Court

Road entrances and listening to the tapping boot-heels of the passers-by.

" My first visit was to the place where I had seen stockings and gloves for sale. It was dark, and I had the devil of a hunt after matches, which I found at last in a drawer of the little cash desk. Then I had to get a candle. I had to tear down wrappers and ransack a number of boxes and drawers, but at last I managed to turn out what I sought: the box label called them lambswool pants and lambs-wool vests. Then socks, a thick comforter, and then I went to the clothing place and got trousers, a lounge jacket, an overcoat, and a slouch hat—a clerical sort of hat with the brim turned down. I began to feel a human being again, and my next thought was food.

" Upstairs was a refreshment department, and there I got cold meat. There was coffee still in the urn, and I lit the gas and warmed it up again, and altogether I did not do badly. Afterwards, prowling through the place in search of blankets—I had to put up at last with a heap of down quilts—I came upon a grocery section with a lot of chocolate and crystallised fruits, more than was good for me, indeed, and some white burgundy. And near that was a toy department, and I had a brilliant idea. I found some artificial noses—dummy noses, you know, and I thought of dark spectacles. But Omnium's had no optical department. My nose had been a difficulty indeed. I had thought of paint. But the discovery set my mind running on wigs and masks, and the like. Finally I went to sleep in a heap of down quilts, very warm and comfortable.

" My last thoughts before sleeping were the most

agreeable I had had since the change. I was in a
state of physical serenity, and that was reflected in
my mind. I thought that I should be able to slip
out unobserved in the morning with my clothes upon
me, muffling my face with a white wrapper I had
taken, purchase spectacles with the money I had
stolen, and so complete my disguise. I lapsed into
disorderly dreams of all the fantastic things that had
happened during the last few days. I saw the ugly
little Jew of a landlord vociferating in his rooms, I
saw his two sons marvelling, and the wrinkled old
woman's gnarled face as she asked for her cat. I
experienced again the strange sensation of seeing
the cloth disappear, and so I came round to the
windy hillside and the sniffing old clergyman
mumbling, ' Earth to earth, ashes to ashes, dust to
dust,' at my father's open grave.

" ' You also,' said a voice, and suddenly I was
being forced towards the grave. I struggled, shouted,
appealed to the mourners, but they continued stonily
following the service; the old clergyman, too, never
faltered, droning and sniffing through the ritual. I
realised I was invisible and inaudible, that overwhelming forces had their grip on me. I struggled
in vain, I was forced over the brink, the coffin rang
hollow as I fell upon it, and the gravel came flying
after me in spadefuls. Nobody heeded me, nobody
was aware of me. I made convulsive struggles and
awoke.

" The pale London dawn had come, the place
was full of a chilly grey light that filtered round the
edges of the window-blinds. I sat up, and for a
time I could not think where this ample apartment,
with its counters, its piles of rolled stuff, its heap of

quilts, and cushions, its iron pillars, might be. Then, as recollection came back to me, I heard voices in conversation.

"Then far down the place, in the brighter light of some department which had already raised its blinds, I saw two men approaching. I scrambled to my feet, looking about me for some way of escape, and even as I did so the sound of my movement made them aware of me. I suppose they saw merely a figure moving quietly and quickly away. 'Who's that?' cried one, and 'Stop there!' shouted the other. I dashed round a corner and came full tilt —a faceless figure, mind you!—on a lanky lad of fifteen. He yelled and I bowled him over, rushed past him, turned another corner, and by a happy inspiration threw myself flat behind a counter. In another moment feet went running past and I heard voices shouting, 'All hands to the doors!' asking what was 'up,' and giving one another advice how to catch me.

"Lying on the ground, I felt scared out of my wits. But, odd as it may seem, it did not occur to me at the moment to take off my clothes, as I should have done. I had made up my mind, I suppose, to get away in them, and that ruled me. And then down the vista of the counters came a bawling of, 'Here he is!'

"I sprang to my feet, whipped a chair off the counter, and sent it whirling at the fool who had shouted, turned, came into another round a corner, sent him spinning, and rushed up the stairs. He kept his footing, gave a view hallo, and came up the staircase hot after me. Up the staircase were piled

a multitude of those bright-coloured pot things—
what are they?"

"Art pots," suggested Kemp.

"That's it! Art pots. Well, I turned at the top
step and swung round, plucked one out of a pile,
and smashed it on his silly head as he came at me.
The whole pile of pots went headlong, and I heard
shouting and footsteps running from all parts. I
made a mad rush for the refreshment place, and
there was a man in white like a man cook, who took
up the chase. I made one last desperate turn and
found myself among lamps and ironmongery. I went
behind the counter of this and waited for my cook,
and as he bolted in at the head of the chase, I
doubled him up with a lamp. Down he went, and
I, crouching behind the counter, began whipping
off my clothes as fast as I could. Coat, jacket,
trousers, shoes, were all right, but a lambswool vest
fits a man like a skin. I heard more men coming,
my cook was lying quiet on the other side of the
counter, stunned or scared speechless, and I had to
make another dash for it, like a rabbit hunted out
of a wood pile.

"'This way, Policeman,' I heard someone shouting. I found myself in my bedstead storeroom again,
and at the end of a wilderness of wardrobes. I
rushed among them, went flat, got rid of my vest
after infinite wriggling, and stood a free man again,
panting and scared, as the policeman and three of
the shopmen came round the corner. They made a
rush for the vest and pants and collared the trousers.
'He's dropping his plunder,' said one of the young
men. 'He *must* be somewhere here.'

"But they did not find me all the same.

" I stood watching them hunt for me for a time, and cursing my ill-luck in losing the clothes. Then I went into the refreshment room, drank a little milk I found there, and sat down by the fire to consider my position.

" In a little while two assistants came in and began to talk over the business very excitedly, and like the fools they were. I heard a magnified account of my depredations, and other speculations as to my whereabouts. Then I fell to scheming again. The insurmountable difficulty of the place, especially now it was alarmed, was to get any plunder out of it. I went down into the warehouse to see if there was any chance of packing and addressing a parcel, but I could not understand the system of checking. About eleven o'clock, the snow having thawed as it fell, and the day being finer and a little warmer than the previous one, I decided that the Emporium was hopeless, and went out again exasperated at my want of success, and with only the vaguest plans of action in my mind.

23

In Drury Lane

" BUT you begin to realise now," said the Invisible Man, " the full disadvantage of my condition. I had no shelter—no covering—to get clothing was to forgo all my advantage, to make of myself a strange and terrible thing. I was fasting; for to eat, to fill myself with unassimilated matter, would be to become grotesquely visible again."

" I never thought of that," said Kemp.

" Nor had I. And the snow had warned me of other dangers. I could not go abroad in snow—it would settle on me and expose me. Rain, too, would make me a watery outline, a glistening surface of a man—a bubble. And fog—I should be like a fainter bubble in a fog, a surface, a greasy glimmer of humanity. Moreover, as I went abroad—in the London air—I gathered dirt about my ankles, floating smuts and dust upon my skin. I did not know how long it would be before I should become visible from that cause also. But I saw clearly it could not be very long."

" Not in London at any rate."

" I went into the slums towards Great Portland Street, and found myself at the end of the street in which I had lodged. I did not go that way because of the crowd half-way down it opposite to the still smoking ruins of the house I had fired. My most immediate problem was to get clothing. Then I saw in one of those little miscellaneous shops—news, sweets, toys, stationery, belated Christmas tomfoolery and so forth—an array of masks and noses, and recalled the idea *Omnium's* toys had suggested. I turned about, no longer aimless, and went circuitously, in order to avoid the busy ways, towards the back streets north of the Strand; for I remembered, though not very distinctly where, that some theatrical costumiers had shops in that district.

" The day was cold, with a nipping wind down the northward running streets. I walked fast to avoid being overtaken. Every crossing was a danger, every passenger a thing to watch alertly. One man, as I was about to pass him at the top of Bedford Street, turned upon me abruptly and came into me, sending me into the road, and almost under the wheel of a passing hansom. The verdict of the cab-rank was that he had had some sort of stroke. I was so unnerved by this encounter that I went into Covent Garden Market and sat down for some time in a quiet corner by a stall of violets, panting and trembling. I found I had caught a fresh cold, and had to turn out after a time lest my sneezes should attract attention.

" At last I reached the object of my quest, a dirty, fly-blown little shop in a by-way near Drury Lane, with a window full of tinsel robes, sham jewels, wigs, slippers, dominoes, and theatrical photographs. The shop was old-fashioned and low and dark, and the house rose above it for four storeys, dark and dismal. I peered through the window, and, seeing no one within, entered. The opening of the door set a clanking bell ringing. I left it open, and walked round a bare costume stand, into a corner behind a cheval glass. For a minute or so no one came. Then I heard heavy feet striding across a room, and a man appeared down the shop.

"My plans were now perfectly definite. I proposed to make my way into the house, secrete myself upstairs, watch my opportunity, and, when everything was quiet, rummage out a wig, mask, spectacles, and costume, and go into the world, perhaps a grotesque but still a creditable figure. And, incidentally, of course, I could rob the house of any available money.

"The man who had entered the shop was a short, slightly hunched, beetle-browed man with long arms and very short bandy legs. Apparently I had interrupted a meal. He stared about the shop with an expression of expectation. This gave way to surprise, and then anger, as he saw the shop empty. 'Damn the boys!' he said. He went to stare up and down the street. He came in again in a minute, kicked the door to with his foot spitefully, and went muttering back to the house door.

"I came forward to follow him, and at the noise of my movement he stopped dead. I did so too, startled by his quickness of ear. He slammed the house door in my face.

"I stood hesitating. Suddenly I heard his quick footsteps returning, and the door re-opened. He stood looking about the shop like one who was still not satisfied. Then, murmuring to himself, he examined the back of the counter and peered behind some fixtures. Then he stood doubtful. He had left the house door open, and I slipped into the inner room.

"It was a queer little room, poorly furnished, and

with a number of big masks in the corner. On the table was his belated breakfast, and it was a confoundedly exasperating thing for me, Kemp, to have to sniff his coffee and stand watching while he came in and resumed his meal. And his table manners were irritating. Three doors opened into the little room, one going upstairs and one down, but they were all shut. I could not get out of the room while he was there; I could scarcely move because of his alertness, and there was a draught down my back. Twice I strangled a sneeze just in time.

"The spectacular quality of my sensations was curious and novel, but for all that I was heartily tired and angry long before he had done his eating. But at last he made an end, and putting his beggarly crockery on the black tin tray upon which he had had his teapot, and gathering all the crumbs up on the mustard-stained cloth, he took the whole lot of things after him. His burden prevented his shutting the door behind him—as he would have done. I never saw such a man for shutting doors—and I followed him into a very dirty underground kitchen and scullery. I had the pleasure of seeing him begin to wash up, and then, finding no good in keeping down there, and the brick floor being cold to my feet, I returned upstairs and sat in his chair by the fire. It was burning low, and scarcely thinking, I put on a little coal. The noise of this brought him up at once, and he stood aglare. He peered about the room and was within an ace of touching me. Even after that examination he scarcely seemed satisfied. He stopped in the doorway and took a final inspection before he went down.

"I waited in the little parlour for an age, and at

last he came up and opened the upstairs door. I crept close after him.

"On the staircase he stopped suddenly, so that I very nearly blundered into him. He stood looking back right into my face, and listening. 'I could have sworn,' he said. His long, hairy hand pulled at his lower lip; his eye went up and down the staircase. Then he grunted, and went on up again.

"His hand was on the handle of a door, and there he stopped again, with the same puzzled anger on his face. He was becoming aware of the faint sound of my movements about him. The man must have had diabolically acute hearing. He suddenly flashed into rage: 'If there's anyone in this house——' he cried, with an oath, and left the threat unfinished. He put his hand in his pocket, failed to find what he wanted, and, rushing past me, went blundering noisily and pugnaciously downstairs. But I did not follow him; I sat on the head of the staircase until his return.

"Presently he came up again, still muttering. He opened the door of the room, and, before I could enter, slammed it in my face.

"I resolved to explore the house, and spent some time in doing so as noiselessly as possible. The house was very old and tumbledown, damp, so that the paper in the attics was peeling from the walls, and rat-infested. Most of the door handles were stiff, and I was afraid to turn them. Several rooms I did inspect were unfurnished, and others were littered with theatrical lumber, bought secondhand, I judged from its appearance. In one room next to his I found a lot of old clothes. I began routing among these, and in my eagerness forgot again the evident sharpness of his ears. I heard a stealthy footstep, and, looking up just in time, saw him peeping in at the tumbled heap and holding an old-fashioned revolver in his hand. I stood perfectly still while he stared about open-mouthed and suspicious. 'It must have been her,' he said slowly. 'Damn her!'

"He shut the door quietly, and immediately I heard the key turn in the lock. Then his footsteps retreated. I realised abruptly that I was locked in. For a minute I did not know what to do. I walked from door to window and back, and stood perplexed. A gust of anger came upon me. But I decided to inspect the clothes before I did anything further, and my first attempt brought down a pile from an upper shelf. This brought him back, more sinister than ever. This time he actually touched me, jumped back with amazement, and stood astonished in the middle of the room.

"Presently he calmed a little. 'Rats,' he said in an undertone, fingers on lip. He was evidently a little scared. I edged quietly out of the room, but a plank creaked. Then the infernal little brute started going all over the house, revolver in hand, and locking door after door and pocketing the keys. When I realised what he was up to I had a fit of rage—I could hardly control myself sufficiently to watch my opportunity. By this time I knew he was alone in the house, and so I made no more ado, but knocked him on the head."

"Knocked him on the head?" exclaimed Kemp.

"Yes—stunned him—as he was going downstairs. Hit him from behind with a stool that stood on the landing. He went downstairs like a bag of old boots."

"But—I say! The common conventions of humanity——"

"Are all very well for common people. But the point was, Kemp, that I had to get out of that house in a disguise without his seeing me. I couldn't think of any other way of doing it. And then I gagged him with a Louis Quatorze vest, and tied him up in a sheet!"

"Tied him up in a sheet!"

"Made a sort of bag of it. It was rather a good idea to keep the idiot scared and quiet, and a devilish hard thing to get out of—head away from the string. My dear Kemp, it's no good your sitting and glaring as though I had done a murder. He had his revolver. If once he had seen me he would have been able to describe me——"

"But still," said Kemp, "in England—to-day! And the man was in his own house, and you were —well, robbing."

"Robbing! Confound it! You'll call me a thief next. Surely, Kemp, you're not fool enough to dance on the old strings. Can't you see my position?"

"And his too!" said Kemp.

The Invisible Man stood up sharply. "What do you mean to say?"

Kemp's face grew a trifle hard. He was about to speak, and checked himself. "I suppose, after all," he said, with a sudden change of manner, "the thing had to be done. You were in a fix. But still——"

"Of course I was in a fix—an infernal fix! And he made me wild too—hunting me about the house,

fooling about with his revolver, locking and un-
locking doors. He was simply exasperating. You
don't blame me, do you? You don't blame me? "

" I never blame anyone," said Kemp. " It's quite
out of fashion. What did you do next? "

" I was hungry. Downstairs I found a loaf and
some rank cheese—more than sufficient to satisfy my
hunger. I took some brandy-and-water, and then
went up past my impromptu bag—he was lying
quite still—to the room containing the old clothes.
This looked out upon the street, two lace curtains,
brown with dirt, guarding the window. I went and
peered out through their interstices. Outside the
day was bright—by contrast with the brown shadows
of the dismal house in which I found myself, dazzlingly
bright. A brisk traffic was going by—fruit carts, a
hansom, a four-wheeler with a pile of boxes, a fish-
monger's cart. I turned with spots of colour
swimming before my eyes to the shadowy fixtures
behind me. My excitement was giving place to a
clear apprehension of my position again. The room
was full of a faint scent of benzoline, used, I suppose,
in cleaning the garments.

" I began a systematic search of the place. I
should judge the hunchback had been alone in the
house for some time. He was a curious person. . . .
Everything that could possibly be of service to me
I collected in the clothes storeroom, and then I made
a deliberate selection. I found a handbag I thought
a suitable possession, and some powder, rouge, and
sticking-plaster.

" I had thought of painting and powdering my
face and all that there was to show of me, in order
to render myself visible, but the disadvantage of this

lay in the fact that I should require turpentine and other appliances and a considerable amount of time before I could vanish again. Finally I chose a nose of the better type, slightly grotesque, but not more so than that of many human beings, dark glasses, greyish whiskers, and a wig. I could find no under-clothing, but that I could buy subsequently, and for the time I swathed myself in calico dominoes and some white cashmere scarves. I could find no socks, but the hunchback's boots were rather a loose fit, and sufficed. In a desk in the shop were three sovereigns and about thirty shillings-worth of silver, and in a locked cupboard I burst in the inner room were eight pounds in gold. I could go forth into the world again, equipped.

" Then came a curious hesitation. Was my appearance really creditable? I tried myself with a little bedroom looking-glass, inspecting myself from every point of view to discover any forgotten chink, but it all seemed sound. I was grotesque to the theatrical pitch—a stage miser—but I was certainly not a physical impossibility. Gathering confidence, I took my looking-glass down into the shop, pulled down the shop blinds, and surveyed myself from every point of view with the help of the cheval glass in the corner.

" I spent some minutes screwing up my courage, and then unlocked the shop door, and marched out into the street, leaving the little man to get out of his sheet again when he liked. In five minutes a dozen turnings intervened between me and the costumier's shop. No one appeared to notice me very pointedly. My last difficulty seemed overcome."

He stopped again.

"And you troubled no more about the hunchback?" said Kemp.

"No," said the Invisible Man. "Nor have I heard what became of him. I suppose he untied himself or kicked himself out. The knots were pretty tight."

He became silent, and went to the window and stared out.

"What happened when you went out into the Strand?"

"Oh! Disillusionment again. I thought my troubles were over. Practically, I thought I had impunity to do whatever I chose, everything—save to give away my secret. So I thought. Whatever I did, whatever the consequences might be, was nothing to me. I had merely to fling aside my garments and vanish. No person could hold me. I could take my money where I found it. I decided to treat myself to a sumptuous feast, and then put up at a good hotel, and accumulate a new outfit of property. I felt amazingly confident; it's not particularly pleasant to recall that I was an ass. I went into a place and was already ordering a lunch, when it occurred to me that I could not eat unless I exposed my invisible face. I finished ordering the lunch, told the man I should be back in ten minutes, and went out exasperated. I don't know if you have ever been disappointed in your appetite."

"Not quite so badly," said Kemp, "but I can imagine it."

"I could have smashed the silly devils. At last, faint with the desire for tasteful food, I went into another place and demanded a private room. 'I am disfigured,' I said, ' badly.' They looked at me curiously, but of course it was not their affair—and so at last I got my lunch. It was not particularly well served, but it sufficed, and when I had had it, I sat over a cigar, trying to plan my line of action. And outside a snow-storm was beginning.

"The more I thought over it, Kemp, the more I realised what a helpless absurdity an Invisible Man was—in a cold and dirty climate and a crowded, civilised city. Before I made this mad experiment I had dreamt of a thousand advantages. That afternoon it seemed all disappointment. I went over the heads of the things a man reckons desirable. No doubt invisibility made it possible to get them, but it made it impossible to enjoy them when they are got. Ambition—what is the good of pride of place when you cannot appear there? What is the good of the love of woman when her name must needs be Delilah? I have no taste for politics, for the blackguardisms of fame, for philanthropy, for sport. What was I to do? And for this I had become a wrapped-up mystery, a swathed and bandaged caricature of a man."

He paused, and his attitude suggested a roving glance at the window.

"But how did you get to Iping?" said Kemp, anxious to keep his guest busy talking.

"I went there to work. I had one hope. It was a half idea! I have it still. It is a full-blown idea now. A way of getting back! Of restoring what I have done. When I choose. When I have done all I mean to do invisibly. And that is what I chiefly want to talk to you about now——"

"You went straight to Iping?"

"Yes. I had simply to get my three volumes of memoranda and my cheque-book, my luggage and underclothing, order a quantity of chemicals to work out this idea of mine—I will show you the calculations as soon as I get my books—and then I started. Jove! I remember the snow-storm now, and the accursed bother it was to keep the snow from damping my pasteboard nose——"

"At the end," said Kemp, "the day before yesterday, when they found you out, you rather— to judge by the papers——"

"I did. Rather. Did I kill that fool of a constable?"

"No," said Kemp. "He's expected to recover."

"That's his luck then. I clean lost my temper, the fools! Why couldn't they leave me alone? And that grocer lout?"

"There's no death expected," said Kemp.

"I don't know about that tramp of mine," said the Invisible Man, with an unpleasant laugh.

"By heaven, Kemp, men of your stamp don't know what rage is! . . . To have worked for years, to have planned and plotted, and then to get some fumbling, purblind idiot messing across your course! . . . Every conceivable sort of silly creature that has ever been created has been sent to cross me. . . . If I have much more of it, I shall go wild—I shall start mowing 'em.

"As it is, they've made things a thousand times more difficult."

24

The Plan that Failed

" BUT now," said Kemp, with a side-glance out of the window, " what are we to do? "

He moved nearer his guest to prevent the possibility of a sudden glimpse of the three men who were advancing up the hill road—with an intolerable slowness, as it seemed to Kemp.

" What were you planning to do, when you were heading for Port Burdock? Had you any plan? "

" I was going to clear out of the country. But I have altered that plan rather since seeing you. I thought it would be wise, now the weather is hot and invisibility possible, to make for the south. Especially as my secret was known, and everyone would be on the look-out for a masked and muffled man. You have a line of steamers from here to France. My idea was to get aboard one and run the risks of the passage. Thence I could go by train into Spain, or else to Algiers. It would not be difficult. There a man might be invisible always, and yet live. And do things. I was using that tramp as a money-box and luggage carrier, until I decided how to get my books and things sent over to meet me."

" That's clear."

" And then the filthy brute must needs try to rob me! He *has* hidden my books, Kemp. Hidden my books!"

" If I can lay my hands on him! . . ."

" Best plan to get the books out of him first."

" But where is he? Do you know? "

" He's in the town police station, locked up, by his own request, in the strongest cell in the place."

" Cur! " said the Invisible Man.

" But that hangs up your plans a little."

" We must get those books; those books are vital."

" Certainly," said Kemp, a little nervously, wondering if he heard footsteps outside. " Certainly we must get those books. But that won't be difficult, if he doesn't know they're for you."

" No," said the Invisible Man, and thought.

·   ·   ·   ·   ·   ·

Kemp tried to think of something to keep the talk going, but the Invisible Man resumed of his own accord.

" Blundering into your house, Kemp," he said, " changes all my plans. For you are a man that can understand. In spite of all that has happened, in spite of this publicity, of the loss of my books, of what I have suffered, there still remain great possibilities, huge possibilities——

" You have told no one I am here? " he asked abruptly.

Kemp hesitated. " That was implied," he said.

" No one? " insisted Griffin.

" Not a soul."

" Ah! Now—— " The Invisible Man stood up, and sticking his arms akimbo, began to pace the study.

" I made a mistake, Kemp, a huge mistake, in

carrying this thing through alone. I have wasted
strength, time, opportunities. Alone; it is wonderful
how little a man can do alone! To rob a little, to
hurt a little, and there is the end.

" What I want, Kemp, is a goal-keeper, a helper,
and a hiding-place; an arrangement whereby I can
sleep and eat and rest in peace and unsuspected. I
must have a confederate. With a confederate, with
food and rest, a thousand things are possible.

" Hitherto I have gone on vague lines. We have
to consider all that invisibility means; all that it
does not mean. It means little advantage for eaves-
dropping and so forth—one makes sounds. It's of
little help—a little help, perhaps—in housebreaking
and so forth. Once you've caught me you could
easily imprison me. But on the other hand I am
hard to catch. This invisibility, in fact, is only good
in two cases. It's useful in getting away; it's useful
in approaching. It's particularly useful, therefore,
in killing. I can walk round a man, whatever
weapon he has, choose my point, strike as I like,
dodge as I like, escape as I like."

Kemp's hand went to his moustache. Was that a
movement downstairs?

" And it is killing we must do, Kemp."

" It is killing we must do," repeated Kemp.
" I'm listening to your plan, Griffin; but I'm not
agreeing, mind. *Why* killing? "

" Not wanton killing, but a judicious slaying. The
point is: They know there is an Invisible Man—as
well as we know there is an Invisible Man—and
that Invisible Man, Kemp, must now establish a
Reign of Terror. Yes; no doubt it's startling, but
I mean it. A Reign of Terror. He must take some

town, like your Burdock, and terrify and dominate
it. He must issue his orders. He can do that in a
thousand ways—scraps of paper thrust under doors
would suffice. And all who disobey his orders he
must kill, and kill all who would defend them."

"Humph!" said Kemp, no longer listening to
Griffin, but to the sound of his front door opening
and closing.

"It seems to me, Griffin," he said, to cover his
wandering attention, "that your confederate would
be in a difficult position?"

"No one would know he was a confederate," said
the Invisible Man eagerly. And then suddenly,
"*Hush!* What's that downstairs?"

"Nothing," said Kemp, and suddenly began to
speak loud and fast. "I don't agree to this, Griffin,"
he said. "Understand me, I don't agree to this.
Why dream of playing a game against the race?
How can you hope to gain happiness? Don't be
a lone wolf. Publish your results—take the world—
take the nation at least into your confidence. Think
what you might do with a million helpers——"

The Invisible Man interrupted—arm extended.
"There are footsteps coming upstairs," he said.

"Nonsense," said Kemp.

"Let me see," said the Invisible Man, and
advanced, arm extended, to the door.

And then things happened very swiftly. Kemp
hesitated for a second, and moved to intercept him.
The Invisible Man started and stood still. "Traitor!"
cried the Voice, and suddenly the dressing-gown
opened, and, sitting down, the unseen began to
disrobe. Kemp made three swift steps to the door,
and forthwith the Invisible Man—his legs had

vanished—sprang to his feet with a shout. Kemp
flung the door open.

As it opened, there came a sound of hurrying
feet downstairs and voices.

With a quick movement Kemp thrust the Invisible
Man back, sprang aside, and slammed the door.
The key was outside and ready. In another moment
Griffin would have been alone in the belvedere
study a prisoner—save for one little thing. The key
had been slipped in hastily that morning. As Kemp
slammed the door it fell noisily upon the carpet.

Kemp's face became white. He tried to grip the
door-handle with both hands. For a moment he
stood lugging. Then the door gave six inches. But
he got it closed again. The second time it was jerked
a foot wide, and the dressing-gown came wedging
itself into the opening. His throat was gripped by
invisible fingers, and he left his hold on the handle
to defend himself. He was forced back, tripped, and
pitched heavily into the corner of the landing. The
empty dressing-gown was flung on the top of him.

Half-way up the staircase was Colonel Adye the
recipient of Kemp's letter, the chief of the Burdock
police. He was staring aghast at the sudden appearance of Kemp, followed by the extraordinary sight
of clothing tossing empty in the air. He saw Kemp
drop and struggle to his feet. He saw Kemp reel,
rush forward, and go down again, felled like an ox.

Then suddenly he was struck violently. By
nothing! A vast weight, it seemed, leapt upon him,
and he was hurled headlong down the staircase, with
a grip on his throat and a knee in his groin. An
invisible foot trod on his back, a ghostly patter
passed downstairs, he heard the two police officers

in the hall shout and run, and the front door of the house slammed violently.

He rolled over and sat up staring. He saw, staggering down the staircase, Kemp, dusty and dishevelled, one side of his face white from a blow, his lip bleeding, and a pink dressing-gown and some other clothing held in his arms.

"My God!" cried Kemp, "the game's up! He's gone!"

25

The Hunting of the Invisible Man

FOR a space Kemp was too inarticulate to make Adye understand the swift things that had just happened. They stood on the landing, Kemp speaking hurriedly, the grotesque swathings of Griffin still on his arm. But presently Adye began to grasp something of the situation.

" He is mad," said Kemp; " inhuman. He is pure selfishness. He thinks of nothing but his own advantage, his own safety. I have listened to such a story this morning of brutal self-seeking. . . . He has wounded men. He will kill them unless we can prevent him. He will create a panic. Nothing can stop him. He is going out now—furious! "

" He must be caught," said Adye. " That is certain."

" But how? " cried Kemp, and suddenly became full of ideas. " You must begin at once; you must set every available man to work; you must prevent his leaving this district. Once he gets away he may go through the countryside as he wills, killing and maiming. He dreams of a reign of terror! A reign of terror, I tell you. You must set a watch on trains and roads and shipping. The garrison must help. You must wire for help. The only thing that may keep him here is the thought of recovering some books of notes he counts of value. I will tell you

of that! There is a man in your police station—
Marvel."

"I know," said Adye, "I know. Those books—
yes. But the tramp. . . ."

"Says he hasn't them. But he thinks the tramp
has. And you must prevent him from eating or
sleeping—day and night the country must be astir
for him. Food must be locked up and secured, all
food, so that he will have to break his way to it.
The houses everywhere must be barred against him.
Heaven send us cold nights and rain! The whole
countryside must begin hunting and keep hunting.
I tell you, Adye, he is a danger, a disaster. Unless
he is pinned down and secured, it is frightful to
think of the things that may happen."

"What else can we do?" said Adye. "I must
go down at once and begin organising. But why not
come? Yes—you come too! Come, and we must
hold a sort of council of war—get Hopps to help—
and the railway managers. By Jove! it's urgent.
Come along—tell me as we go. What else is there
we can do? Put that stuff down."

In another moment Adye was leading the way
downstairs. They found the front door open and
the policemen standing outside staring at empty air.
"He's got away, sir," said one.

"We must go to the central station at once," said
Adye. "One of you go on down and get a cab to
come up and meet us—quickly. And now, Kemp,
what else?"

"Dogs," said Kemp. "Get dogs. They don't see
him, but they wind him. Get dogs."

"Good," said Adye. "It's not generally known,

but the prison officials over at Halstead know a man
with bloodhounds. Dogs. What else? "

"Bear in mind," said Kemp, "his food shows.
After eating, his food shows until it is assimilated.
So that he has to hide after eating. You must keep
on beating. Every thicket, every quiet corner. And
put all weapons—all implements that might be
weapons, away. He can't carry such things for long.
And what he can snatch up and strike men with
must be hidden away."

"Good again," said Adye. "We shall have him
yet! "

"And on the roads——" said Kemp, and
hesitated.

"Yes? " said Adye.

"Powdered glass," said Kemp. "It's cruel, I
know. But think of what he may do! "

Adye drew the air in between his teeth sharply.
"It's unsportsmanlike. I don't know. But I'll have
powdered glass got ready. If he goes too far. . . ."

"The man's become inhuman, I tell you," said
Kemp. "I am sure he will establish a reign of
terror—so soon as he has got over the emotions of
this escape—as I am sure I am talking to you. Our
only chance is to be ahead. He has cut himself off
from his kind. His blood be upon his own head."

26

The Wicksteed Murder

THE Invisible Man seems to have rushed out of Kemp's house in a state of blind fury. A little child playing near Kemp's gateway was violently caught up and thrown aside, so that its ankle was broken —and thereafter for some hours he passed out of human perceptions. No one knows where he went nor what he did. But one can imagine him hurrying through the hot June forenoon, up the hill and on to the open downland behind Port Burdock, raging and despairing at his intolerable fate, and sheltering at last, heated and weary, amid the thickets of Hintondean, to piece together again his shattered schemes against his species. That seems the most probable refuge for him, for there it was he reasserted himself in a grimly tragical manner about two in the afternoon.

One wonders what his state of mind may have been during that time and what plans he devised. No doubt he was almost ecstatically exasperated by Kemp's treachery, and though we may be able to understand the motives that led to that deceit, we may still imagine, and even sympathise a little with the fury the attempted surprise must have occasioned. Perhaps something of the stunned astonishment of his Oxford Street experiences may have returned to him, for evidently he had counted on Kemp's co-operation in his brutal dream of a terrorised world.

At any rate, he vanished from human ken about midday, and no living witness can tell what he did until about half-past two. It was a fortunate thing, perhaps, for humanity, but for him it was a fatal inaction.

During that time a growing multitude of men scattered over the countryside were busy. In the morning he had still been simply a legend, a terror; in the afternoon, by virtue chiefly of Kemp's dryly worded proclamation, he was presented as a tangible antagonist, to be wounded, captured, or overcome, and the countryside began organising itself with inconceivable rapidity. By two o'clock even, he might still have removed himself out of the district by getting aboard a train, but after two that became impossible, every passenger train along the lines on a great parallelogram between Southampton, Winchester, Brighton and Horsham, travelled with locked doors, and the goods traffic was almost entirely suspended. And in a great circle of twenty miles round Port Burdock men armed with guns and bludgeons were presently setting out in groups of three and four, with dogs, to beat roads and fields.

Mounted policemen rode along the country lanes, stopping at every cottage and warning the people to lock up their houses and keep indoors unless they were armed, and all the elementary schools had broken up by three o'clock, and the children, scared and keeping together in groups, were hurrying home. Kemp's proclamation—signed, indeed, by Adye—was posted over almost the whole district by four or five o'clock in the afternoon. It gave briefly but clearly all the conditions of the struggle, the necessity of keeping the Invisible Man from food and sleep,

the necessity for incessant watchfulness, and for a
prompt attention to any evidence of his movements.
And so swift and decided was the action of the
authorities, so prompt and universal was the belief
in this strange being, that before nightfall an area
of several hundred square miles was in a stringent
state of siege. And before nightfall, too, a thrill of
horror went through the whole watching, nervous
countryside, and going from whispering mouth to
mouth, swift and certain over the length and breadth
of the country passed the story of the murder of
Mr. Wicksteed.

If our supposition that the Invisible Man's refuge
was the Hintondean thickets is correct, then we must
suppose that in the early afternoon he sallied out
again, bent upon some project that involved the use
of a weapon. We cannot know what the project was,
but the evidence that he had the iron rod in his
hand before he met Wicksteed is to me, at least,
overwhelming.

Of course we can know nothing of the details of
that encounter. It occurred on the edge of a gravel
pit, not two hundred yards from Lord Burdock's
lodge gate. Everything points to a desperate struggle
—the trampled ground, the numerous wounds Mr.
Wicksteed received, his splintered walking-stick—
but why the attack was made, save in a murderous
frenzy, it is impossible to imagine. Indeed, the
theory of madness is almost unavoidable. Mr. Wicksteed was a man of forty-five or forty-six, steward
to Lord Burdock, of inoffensive habits and appearance, and the very last person in the world to
provoke such a terrible antagonist. Against him it
would seem the Invisible Man used an iron rod,

dragged from a piece of broken fence. He stopped this quiet man, going quietly home to his midday meal, attacked him, beat down his feeble defences, broke his arm, felled him, and smashed his head to a jelly.

Of course, he must have dragged this rod out of the fencing, before he met his victim—he must have been carrying it ready in his hand. Only two details beyond what has already been stated seem to bear on the matter. One is the circumstance that the gravel-pit was not in Mr. Wicksteed's direct path home, but nearly a couple of hundred yards out of his way. The other is the assertion of a little girl, to the effect that going to her afternoon school she saw the murdered man "*trotting*" in a peculiar manner across a field towards the gravel-pit. Her pantomime of his action suggests a man pursuing something on the ground before him and striking at it ever and again with his walking stick. She was the last person to see him alive. He passed out of her sight to his death, the struggle being hidden from her only by a clump of beech trees and a slight depression in the ground.

Now this, to the present writer's mind at least, certainly lifts the murder out of the realm of the absolutely wanton. We may imagine that Griffin had taken the rod as a weapon indeed, but without any deliberate intention of using it to murder. Wicksteed may then have come by and noticed this rod inexplicably moving through the air. Without any thought of the Invisible Man—for Port Burdock is ten miles away—he may have pursued it. It is quite conceivable that he may not even have heard of the Invisible Man. One can, then, imagine the

Invisible Man making off quietly in order to avoid discovering his presence in the neighbourhood, and Wicksteed, excited and curious, pursuing this unaccountably locomotive object, finally striking at it.

No doubt the Invisible Man could easily have distanced his middle-aged pursuer under ordinary circumstances, but the position in which Wicksteed's body was found suggests that he had the ill-luck to drive his quarry into a corner between a drift of stinging nettles and the gravel-pit. To those who appreciate the extraordinary irascibility of the Invisible Man the rest of the encounter will be easy to imagine.

But this is a pure hypothesis. The only undeniable facts—for stories of children are often unreliable—are the discovery of Wicksteed's body, done to death, and of the blood-stained iron rod flung among the nettles. The abandonment of the rod by Griffin suggests that in the emotional excitement of the affair the purpose for which he took it—if he had a purpose—was abandoned. He was certainly an intensely egotistical and unfeeling man, but the sight of his victim, his first victim, bloody and pitiful at his feet, may have released some long pent fountain of remorse to flood for a time whatever scheme of action he had contrived.

After the murder of Mr. Wicksteed, he would seem to have struck across the country towards the downland. There is a story of a voice heard about sunset by a couple of men in a field near Fern Bottom. It was wailing and laughing, sobbing and groaning, and ever and again it shouted. It must have been queer hearing. It drove up across the middle of a clover field and died away towards the hills.

In the interim the Invisible Man must have learnt something of the rapid use Kemp had made of his confidences. He must have found houses locked and secured, he may have loitered about railway stations and prowled about inns, and no doubt he read the proclamations and realised something of the nature of the campaign against him. And as the evening advanced the fields became dotted here and there with groups of three or four men, and noisy with the yelping of dogs. These men-hunters had particular instructions in the case of an encounter as to the way they should support one another. But he avoided them all. We may understand something of his exasperation, and it could have been none the less because he himself had supplied the information that was being used so remorselessly against him. For that day at least he lost heart; for nearly twenty-four hours, save when he turned on Wicksteed, he was a hunted man. In the night he must have eaten and slept, for in the morning he was himself again, active, powerful, angry and malignant, prepared for his last great struggle against the world.

27

The Siege of Kemp's House

KEMP read a strange missive, written in pencil on
a greasy sheet of paper.

" You have been amazingly energetic and clever,"
this letter ran, " though what you stand to gain by
it I cannot imagine. You are against me. For a
whole day you have chased me—you have tried to
rob me of a night's rest. But I have had food in
spite of you, I have slept in spite of you, and the
game is only beginning. The game is only beginning.
There is nothing for it but to start the Terror. This
announces the first day of the Terror. Port Burdock
is no longer under the Queen, tell your Colonel of
Police, and the rest of them; it is under me—the
Terror! This is day one of year one of the new
epoch—the Epoch of the Invisible Man. I am
Invisible Man the First. To begin with, the rule
will be easy. The first day there will be one execution
for the sake of example—a man named Kemp.
Death starts for him to-day. He may lock himself
away, hide himself away, get guards about him, put
on armour if he likes—Death, the unseen Death, is
coming. Let him take precautions—it will impress
my people. Death starts from the pillar-box by
midday. The letter will fall in as the postman comes
along, then off! The game begins. Death starts.
Help him not, my people, lest Death fall upon you
also. To-day Kemp is to die."

Kemp read this letter twice. "It's no hoax," he said. "That's his voice! And he means it."

He turned the folded sheet over and saw on the addressed side of it the postmark Hintondean and the prosaic detail, " 2*d. to pay.*"

He got up slowly, leaving his lunch unfinished— the letter had come by the one o'clock post—and went into his study. He rang for his housekeeper, and told her to go round the house at once, examine all the fastenings of the windows, and close all the shutters. He closed the shutters of his study himself. From a locked drawer in his bedroom he took a little revolver, examined it carefully, and put it into the pocket of his lounge jacket. He wrote a number of brief notes, one to Colonel Adye, gave them to his servant to take, with explicit instructions as to her way of leaving the house. "There is no danger," he said, and added a mental reservation, "to you." He remained meditative for a space after doing this, and then returned to his cooling lunch.

He ate with gaps of thought. Finally he struck the table sharply. "We will have him!" he said, "and I am the bait. He will come too far."

He went up to the belvedere, carefully shutting every door after him. "It's a game," he said, "an odd game—but the chances are all for me, Mr. Griffin, in spite of your invisibility. And pluck. Griffin *contra mundum* . . . with a vengeance!"

He stood at the window staring at the hot hillside. "He must get food every day—and I don't envy him. Did he really sleep last night? Out in the open somewhere—secure from collisions. I wish we could get some good cold, wet weather instead of the heat.

" He may be watching me now."

He went close to the window. Something rapped smartly against the brickwork over the frame, and made him start violently back.

" I'm getting nervous," said Kemp. But it was five minutes before he went to the window again. " It must have been a sparrow," he said.

Presently he heard the front-door bell ringing and hurried downstairs. He unbolted and unlocked the door, examined the chain, put it up, and opened cautiously without showing himself. A familiar voice hailed him. It was Adye. " Your servant's been assaulted, Kemp," he said round the door.

" What! " exclaimed Kemp.

" Had that note of yours taken away from her. He's close about here. Let me in."

Kemp released the chain, and Adye entered through as narrow an opening as possible. He stood in the hall, looking with infinite relief at Kemp refastening the door. " Note was snatched out of her hand. Scared her horribly. She's down at the station. Hysterics. He's close here. What was it about? "

Kemp swore.

" What a fool I was! " said Kemp. " I might have known. It's not an hour's walk from Hinton-dean. Already! "

" What's up? " said Adye.

" Look here! " said Kemp, and led the way into his study. He handed Adye the Invisible Man's letter. Adye read it, and whistled softly. " And you——? " said Adye.

" Proposed a trap—like a fool," said Kemp,

" and sent my proposal out by a maidservant. To him."

Adye followed Kemp's profanity.

" He'll clear out," said Adye.

" Not him," said Kemp.

A resounding smash of glass came from upstairs. Adye had a silvery glimpse of a little revolver half out of Kemp's pocket. " It's a window upstairs! " said Kemp, and led the way up. There came a second crash while they were still on the staircase. When they reached the study they found two of the three windows smashed, half the room littered with splintered glass, and one big flint lying on the writing-table. The two men stopped in the doorway contemplating the wreckage. Kemp swore again, and as he did so the third window went with a snap like a pistol, hung starred for a moment, and collapsed in jagged, shivering triangles into the room.

" What's this for? " said Adye.

" It's a beginning," said Kemp.

" There's no way of climbing up here? "

" Not for a cat," said Kemp.

" No shutters? "

" Not here. All the downstairs rooms—Hallo! " Smash, and then the whack of boards hit hard came from downstairs. " Confound him! " said Kemp. " That must be—yes—it's one of the bed-rooms. He's going to do all the house. But he's a fool. The shutters are up and the glass will fall outside. He'll cut his feet."

Another window proclaimed its destruction. The two men stood on the landing perplexed.

" I have it! " said Adye. " Let me have a stick

or something, and I'll go down to the station and get the bloodhounds put on. That ought to settle him! "

Another window went the way of its fellows.

" You haven't a revolver? " asked Adye.

Kemp's hand went to his pocket. Then he hesitated. " I haven't one—at least to spare."

" I'll bring it back," said Adye. " You'll be safe here."

Kemp, ashamed of his momentary lapse from truthfulness, handed him the weapon.

" Now for the door," said Adye.

As they stood hesitating in the hall, they heard one of the first-floor bedroom windows crack and clash. Kemp went to the door and began to slip the bolts as silently as possible. His face was a little paler than usual.

" You must step straight out," said Kemp.

In another moment Adye was on the doorstep and the bolts were dropping back into the staples. He hesitated for a moment, feeling more comfortable with his back against the door. Then he marched, upright and square, down the steps. He crossed the lawn and approached the gate. A little breeze seemed to ripple over the grass. Something moved near him.

" Stop a bit," said a Voice, and Adye stopped dead, and his hand tightened on the revolver.

" Well? " said Adye, white and grim, and every nerve tense.

" Oblige me by going back to the house," said the Voice, as tense and grim as Adye's.

" Sorry," said Adye, a little hoarsely, and moistened his lips with his tongue. The Voice was on his left front, he thought; suppose he were to take his luck with a shot?

"What are you going for?" said the Voice, and there was a quick movement of the two, and a flash of sunlight from the open lip of Adye's pocket.

Adye desisted and thought. "Where I go," he said slowly, "is my own business." The words were still on his lips, when an arm came round his neck, his back felt a knee, and he was sprawling backward. He drew clumsily and fired absurdly, and in another moment he was struck in the mouth and the revolver wrested from his grip. He made a vain clutch at a slippery limb, tried to struggle up and fell back. "Damn!" said Adye. The Voice laughed.

"I'd kill you now if it wasn't the waste of a bullet," it said. He saw the revolver in mid-air, six feet off, covering him.

"Well?" said Adye, sitting up.

"Get up," said the Voice.

Adye stood up.

"Attention!" said the Voice, and then firmly, "don't try any games. Remember I can see your face, if you can't see mine. You've got to go back to the house."

"He won't let me in," said Adye.

"That's a pity," said the Invisible Man. "I've got no quarrel with you."

Adye moistened his lips again. He glanced away from the barrel of the revolver, and saw the sea far off, very blue and dark under the midday sun, the smooth green down, the white cliff of the head, and the multitudinous town, and suddenly he knew that life was very sweet. His eyes came back to this little metal thing hanging between heaven and earth, six yards away. "What am I to do?" he said sullenly.

"What am *I* to do?" asked the Invisible Man. "You will get help. The only thing is for you to go back."

"I will try. If he lets me in will you promise not to rush the door?"

"I've got no quarrel with you," said the Voice.

Kemp had hurried upstairs after letting Adye out, and now, crouching among the broken glass, and peering cautiously over the edge of the study window-sill, he saw Adye stand parleying with the unseen. "Why doesn't he fire?" whispered Kemp to himself. Then the revolver moved a little, and the glint of the sunlight flashed in Kemp's eyes. He shaded his eyes and tried to see the course of the blinding beam.

"Surely!" he said. "Adye has given up the revolver."

"Promise not to rush the door," Adye was saying. "Don't push a winning game too far. Give a man a chance."

"You go back to the house. I tell you flatly I will not promise anything."

Adye's decision seemed suddenly made. He turned towards the house, walking slowly with his hands behind him. Kemp watched him—puzzled. The revolver vanished, flashed again into sight, vanished again, and became evident on a closer scrutiny as a little dark object following Adye. Then things happened very quickly. Adye leapt backwards, swung round, clutched at this little object, missed it, threw up his hands and fell forward on his face, leaving a little puff of blue in the air.

Kemp did not hear the sound of the shot. Adye writhed, raised himself on one arm, fell forward, and lay still.

For a space Kemp remained staring at the quiet carelessness of Adye's attitude. The afternoon was very hot and still, nothing seemed stirring in all the world save a couple of yellow butterflies chasing each other through the shrubbery between the house and the road gate. Adye lay on the lawn near the gate. The blinds of all the villas down the hill road were drawn, but in one little green summer-house was a white figure, apparently an old man asleep. Kemp scrutinised the surroundings of the house for a glimpse of the revolver, but it had vanished. His eyes came back to Adye—— The game was opening well.

Then came a ringing and knocking at the front door, that grew at last tumultuous, but, pursuant to Kemp's instructions, the servants had locked themselves into their rooms. This was followed by a silence. Kemp sat listening and then began peering cautiously out of the three windows, one after another. He went to the staircase head and stood listening uneasily. He armed himself with his bed-room poker, and went to examine the interior fastenings of the ground-floor windows again. Everything was safe and quiet. He returned to the belvedere. Adye lay motionless over the edge of the gravel just as he had fallen. Coming along the road by the villas were the housemaid and two policemen.

Everything was deadly still. The three people seemed very slow in approaching. He wondered what his antagonist was doing.

He started. There was a smash from below. He hesitated and went downstairs again. Suddenly the house resounded with heavy blows and the splintering of wood. He heard a smash and the distinctive clang of the iron fastenings of shutters. He turned the key and opened the kitchen door. As he did so the shutters, split and splintering, came flying inward. He stood aghast. The window frame, save for one cross-bar, was still intact, but only little teeth of glass remained in the frame. The shutters had been driven in with an axe, and now the axe was descending in sweeping blows upon the window frame and the iron bars defending it. Then suddenly it leapt aside and vanished.

He saw the revolver lying on the path outside, and then the little weapon sprang into the air. He dodged back. The revolver cracked just too late, and a splinter from the edge of the closing door flashed over his head. He slammed and locked the door, and as he stood outside he heard Griffin shouting and laughing. Then the blows of the axe with their splitting and smashing accompaniments were resumed.

Kemp stood in the passage trying to think. In a moment the Invisible Man would be in the kitchen. This door would not keep him a moment, and then——

A ringing came at the front door again. It would be the policemen. He ran into the hall, put up the chain, and drew the bolts. He made the girl speak before he dropped the chain, and the three people blundered into the house in a heap, and Kemp slammed the door again.

" The Invisible Man! " said Kemp. " He has a

revolver with two shots—left. He's killed Adye. Shot him anyhow. Didn't you see him on the lawn? He's lying there."

" Who? " said one of the policemen.

" Adye," said Kemp.

" We came round the back way," said the girl.

" What's that smashing? " asked one of the policemen.

" He's in the kitchen—or will be. He has found an axe——"

Suddenly the house was full of the Invisible Man's resounding blows on the kitchen door. The girl stared towards the kitchen and stepped into the dining-room. Kemp tried to explain in broken sentences. They heard the kitchen door give.

" This way," cried Kemp, bursting into activity, and bundled the policemen into the dining-room doorway.

" Poker," said Kemp, and rushed to the fender.

He handed the poker he had carried to one policeman, and the dining-room one to the other.

He suddenly flung himself backward. " Whup," said one policeman, ducked, and caught the axe on his poker. The pistol snapped its penultimate shot and ripped a valuable Sidney Cooper. The second policeman brought his poker down on the little weapon, as one might knock down a wasp, and sent it rattling to the floor.

At the first clash the girl screamed, stood screaming for a moment by the fireplace, and then ran to open the shutters—possibly with an idea of escaping by the shattered window.

The axe receded into the passage and fell to a position about two feet from the ground. They could hear the Invisible Man breathing. " Stand away you two," he said. " I want that man Kemp."

" We want you," said the first policeman, making a quick step forward and wiping with his poker at the Voice. The Invisible Man must have started back, and he blundered into the umbrella stand.

Then, as the policeman staggered with the swing of the blow he had aimed, the Invisible Man countered with the axe, the helmet crumpled like paper, and the blow sent the man spinning to the floor at the head of the kitchen stairs.

But the second policeman, aiming behind the axe with his poker, hit something soft that snapped. There was a sharp exclamation of pain, and then the axe fell to the ground. The policeman wiped again at vacancy and hit nothing; he put his foot on the axe and struck again. Then he stood, poker clubbed, listening, intent for the slightest movement.

He heard the dining-room window open, and a quick rush of feet within. His companion rolled over and sat up, with the blood running down between his eye and ear. " Where is he? " asked the man on the floor.

" Don't know. I've hit him. He's standing somewhere in the hall unless he's slipped past you. Dr. Kemp—sir! "

" Dr. Kemp," cried the policeman again.

The second policeman began struggling to his feet. He stood up. Suddenly the faint pad of bare feet on the kitchen stairs could be heard. " Yap! " cried the first policeman, and flung his poker. It smashed a little gas-bracket.

He made as if he would pursue the Invisible Man

downstairs. Then he thought better of it, and stepped into the dining-room.

" Dr. Kemp——" he began, and stopped short.

" Dr. Kemp's a hero," he said, as his companion looked over his shoulder.

The dining-room window was wide open, and neither handmaid nor Kemp was to be seen.

The second policeman's opinion of Kemp was terse and vivid.

28

The Hunter Hunted

MR. HEELAS, Mr. Kemp's nearest neighbour among the villa holders, was asleep in his summer-house when the siege of Kemp's house began. Mr. Heelas was one of the sturdy majority who refused to believe in " all this nonsense " about an Invisible Man. His wife, however, as he was to be reminded subsequently, did. He insisted upon walking about his garden just as if nothing was the matter, and he went to sleep in the afternoon, in accordance with the custom of years. He slept through the smashing of the windows, and then woke up suddenly, with a curious persuasion of something wrong. He looked across at Kemp's house, rubbed his eyes, and looked again. Then he put his feet to the ground and sat listening. He said he was damned, but still the strange thing was visible. The house looked as though it had been deserted for weeks—after a violent riot. Every window was broken, and every window, save those of the belvedere study, was blinded by internal shutters.

" I could have sworn it was all right "—he looked at his watch—" twenty minutes ago."

He became aware of a measured concussion, and the clash of glass far away in the distance. And then, as he sat open-mouthed, came a still more wonderful thing. The shutters of the dining-room window were flung open violently, and the housemaid, in her outdoor hat and garments, appeared struggling in a frantic manner to throw up the sash. Suddenly a man appeared beside her, helping her—Dr. Kemp! In another moment the window was open and the housemaid was struggling out; she pitched forward and vanished among the shrubs. Mr. Heelas stood up, exclaiming vaguely and vehemently at all these wonderful things. He saw Kemp stand on the sill, spring from the window, and reappear almost instantaneously running along a path in the shrubbery and stooping as he ran, like a man who evades observation. He vanished behind a laburnum, and appeared again clambering a fence that abutted on the open down. In a second he had tumbled over, and was running at a tremendous pace down the slope towards Mr. Heelas.

"Lord!" cried Mr. Heelas, struck with an idea, "it's that Invisible Man brute! It's all right after all!"

With Mr. Heelas to think things like that was to act, and his cook, watching him from the top window, was amazed to see him come pelting towards the house at a good nine miles an hour. There was a slamming of doors, a ringing of bells, and the voice of Mr. Heelas bellowing like a bull. "Shut the doors, shut the windows, shut everything —the Invisible Man is coming!" Instantly the house was full of screams and directions and scurrying feet. He himself ran to shut the french windows that opened on the veranda, and as he did so Kemp's head and shoulders and knee appeared over the edge of the garden fence. In another moment Kemp had ploughed through the asparagus, and was running across the tennis-lawn to the house.

" You can't come in," said Mr. Heelas, shooting the bolts. " I'm very sorry if he's after you—but you can't come in! "

Kemp appeared with a face of terror close to the glass, rapping and then shaking frantically at the french window. Then, seeing his efforts were useless, he ran along the veranda, vaulted the end, and went to hammer at the side door. Then he ran round by the side gate to the front of the house, and so into the hill road. And Mr. Heelas staring from his window—a face of horror—had scarcely witnessed Kemp vanish ere the asparagus was being trampled this way and that by feet unseen. At that Mr. Heelas fled precipitately upstairs, and the rest of the chase is beyond his purview. But as he passed the stair-case window he heard the side gate slam.

Emerging into the hill road, Kemp naturally took the downward direction, and so it was that he came to run in his own person the very race he had watched with such a critical eye from the belvedere study only four days ago. He ran it well for a man out of training, and though his face was white and wet his wits were cool to the last. He ran with wide strides, and wherever a patch of rough ground intervened, wherever there came a patch of raw flints, or a bit of broken glass shone dazzling, he crossed it, and left the bare invisible feet that followed to take what line they would.

For the first time in his life Kemp discovered that the hill road was indescribably vast and desolate, and that the beginnings of the town far below at the hill foot were strangely remote. Never had there been a slower or more painful method of progression than running. All the gaunt villas, sleeping in the

afternoon sun, looked locked and barred; no doubt
they were locked and barred by his own orders. But
at any rate they might have kept a look-out for an
eventuality like this! The town was rising up now,
the sea had dropped out of sight behind it, and
people below were stirring. A tram was just arriving
at the hill foot. Beyond that was the police station.
Were those footsteps he heard behind him? Spurt.

The people below were staring at him, one or
two were running, and his breath was beginning
to saw in his throat. The tram was quite near now,
and the " Jolly Cricketers " was noisily barring its
doors. Beyond the tram were posts and heaps of
gravel—the drainage works. He had a transitory
idea of jumping into the tram and slamming the
doors, and then he resolved to go for the police
station. In another moment he had passed the door
of the " Jolly Cricketers," and was in the blistering
fag end of the street, with human beings about him.
The tram driver and his helper—astounded by the
sight of his furious haste—stood staring with the
tram horses unhitched. Farther on the astonished
features of navvies appeared above the mounds of
gravel.

His pace broke a little, and then he heard the
swift pad of his pursuer, and leapt forward again.
" The Invisible Man! " he cried to the navvies, with
a vague indicative gesture, and by an inspiration
leapt the excavation, and placed a burly group
between him and the chase. Then, abandoning the
idea of the police station, he turned into a little
side street, rushed by a greengrocer's cart, hesitated
for the tenth of a second at the door of a sweet-stuff
shop, and then made for the mouth of an alley that

ran back into the main Hill Street again. Two or
three little children were playing here, and shrieked
and scattered running at his apparition, and forthwith, doors and windows opened, and excited
mothers revealed their hearts. Out he shot into Hill
Street once more, three hundred yards from the
tram-line end, and immediately he became aware
of a tumultuous vociferation and running people.

He glanced up the street towards the hill. Hardly
a dozen yards off ran a huge navvy, cursing in
fragments and slashing viciously with a spade, and
hard behind him came the tram conductor with his
fists clenched. Up the street others followed these
two, striking and shouting. Down towards the town
men and women were running, and he noticed
clearly one man coming out of a shop door with a
stick in his hand. " Spread out! Spread out! " cried
someone. Kemp suddenly grasped the altered condition of the chase. He stopped and looked round,
panting. " He's close here! " he cried. " Form a
line across——"

He was hit hard under the ear, and went reeling,
trying to face round towards his unseen antagonist.
He just managed to keep his feet, and he struck a
vain counter in the air. Then he was hit again
under the jaw, and sprawled headlong on the
ground. In another moment a knee compressed
his diaphragm, and a couple of eager hands gripped
his throat, but the grip of one was weaker than the
other; he grasped the wrists, heard a cry of pain
from his assailant, and then the spade of the navvy
came whirling through the air above him, and
struck something with a dull thud. He felt a drop
of moisture on his face. The grip at his throat

suddenly relaxed, and with a convulsive effort Kemp loosed himself, grasped a limp shoulder, and rolled uppermost. He gripped the unseen elbows near the ground. " I've got him! " screamed Kemp. " Help! help—hold! He's down! Hold his feet! "

In another second there was a simultaneous rush upon the struggle, and a stranger coming into the road suddenly might have thought an exceptionally savage game of Rugby football was in progress. And there was no shouting after Kemp's cry—only a sound of blows and feet and a heavy breathing.

Then came a mighty effort, and the Invisible Man staggered to his feet. Kemp clung to him in front like a hound to a stag, and a dozen hands clutched and tore at the unseen. The tram conductor got the neck, and lugged him back.

Down went the heap of struggling men again. There was, I am afraid, some savage kicking. Then suddenly a wild scream of " Mercy, mercy! " that died down swiftly to a sound like choking.

" Get back, you fools! " cried the muffled voice of Kemp, and there was a vigorous shoving back of stalwart forms. " He's hurt, I tell you. Stand back."

There was a brief struggle to clear a space, and then the circle of eager faces saw the doctor kneeling, as it seemed, fifteen inches in the air, and holding invisible arms to the ground. Behind him a constable gripped invisible ankles.

" Don't you leave go of en! " cried the big navvy, holding a bloodstained spade; " he's shamming."

" He's not shamming," said the doctor, cautiously raising his knee, " and I'll hold him." His face was bruised, and already turning red; he spoke thickly, because of a bleeding lip. He released one hand, and seemed to be feeling at the face. "The mouth's all wet," he said. And then, "Good Lord!"

He stood up abruptly, and then knelt down on the ground by the side of the thing unseen. There was a pushing and shuffling, a sound of heavy feet as fresh people came to increase the pressure of the crowd. Men were coming out of the houses. The doors of the "Jolly Cricketers" stood suddenly wide open. Very little was said. Kemp felt about, his hand seeming to pass through empty air. "He's not breathing," he said, and then, "I can't feel his heart. His side—ugh!"

An old woman, peering under the arm of the big navvy, screamed sharply. "Looky here!" she said, and thrust out a wrinkled finger. And looking where she pointed, everyone saw, faint and transparent, as though made of glass, so that veins and arteries, and bones and nerves could be distinguished, the outline of a hand—a hand limp and prone. It grew clouded and opaque even as they stared.

"Hallo!" cried the constable. "Here's his feet a-showing!"

And so, slowly, beginning at his hands and feet, and creeping slowly along his limbs to the vital centres of his body, that strange change to visible fleshliness continued. It was like the slow spreading of a poison. First came the little white veins tracing a hazy grey sketch of a limb, then the glassy bones and intricate arteries, then the flesh and skin, first a faint fogginess and then growing rapidly dense and opaque. Presently they could see his crushed chest and his shoulders, and the dim outline of his drawn and battered features.

When at last the crowd made way for Kemp to stand erect, there lay, naked and pitiful on the ground, the bruised and broken body of a young man about thirty. His hair and brow were white—not grey with age, but white with the whiteness of albinism—and his eyes were like garnets. His hands were clenched, his eyes wide open, and his expression was one of anger and dismay.

" Cover his face! " cried a man. " For Gawd's sake cover that face! "

Some one brought a sheet from the " Jolly Cricketers," and having covered him, they carried him into the house. And there it was, on a shabby bed in a tawdry, ill-lighted bedroom, surrounded by a crowd of ignorant and excited people, broken and wounded, betrayed and unpitied, that Griffin, the first of all men to make himself invisible, Griffin, the most gifted physicist the world has ever seen, ended in infinite disaster his strange and terrible career.

THE EPILOGUE

So ends the story of the strange and evil experiment of the Invisible Man. And if you would learn more of him you must go to a little inn near Port Stowe and talk to the landlord. The sign of the inn is an empty board save for a hat and boots, and the name is the title of this story. The landlord is a short and corpulent little man with a nose of cylindrical protrusion, wiry hair, and a sporadic rosiness of visage. Drink generously, and he will tell you generously of all the things that happened to him after that time, and of how the lawyers tried to " do him out of " the treasure found upon him.

"When they found they couldn't prove who's money was which, I'm blessed," he says, " if they didn't try to make me out a blooming treasure trove! Do I *look* like a Treasure Trove? And then a gentleman gave me a guinea a night to tell the story at the Empire Music 'All—just tell 'em in my own words—barring one."

And if you want to cut off the flow of his reminiscences abruptly, you can always do so by asking if there weren't three manuscript books in the story. He admits there were, and proceeds to explain with asseverations that everybody thinks *he* has 'em. But, bless you! he hasn't. "The Invisible Man it was took 'em off to hide 'em when I cut and ran for Port Stowe. It's that Mr. Kemp put people on with the idea of *my* having 'em."

He subsides into a pensive state, watches you furtively, bustles nervously with glasses, and presently leaves the bar.

He is a bachelor man—his tastes were ever bachelor, and there are no women folk in the house. Outwardly he buttons—it is expected of him—but in his more vital privacies, in the matter of braces, for example, he still turns to string. He conducts his house without enterprise, but with eminent decorum. His movements are slow, and he is a great thinker. But he has a reputation for wisdom and for a respectable parsimony in the village, and his knowledge of the roads of the South of England would beat Cobbett.

On Sunday mornings, every Sunday morning, all the year round, while he is closed to the outer world, and every night after ten, he goes into his bar parlour, bearing a glass of gin faintly tinged with water, and having placed this down, he locks the door and examines the blinds, and even looks under the table. And then, being satisfied of his solitude, he unlocks the cupboard, and a box in the cupboard, and a drawer in that box, and produces three volumes bound in brown leather, and places them solemnly in the middle of the table. The covers are weather-worn and tinged with an algal green—for once they sojourned in a ditch, and some of the pages have been washed blank by dirty water. The landlord sits down in an arm-chair, fills a long clay pipe slowly—gloating over the books the while. Then he pulls one towards him and begins to study it, turning over the leaves backwards and forwards.

His brows are knit and his lips move painfully.

"Hex, little two up in the air, cross and a fiddle-de-dee. Lord! what a one he was for intellect!"

Presently he relaxes and leans back, and blinks through his smoke across the room at things invisible to other eyes. "Full of secrets," he says. "Wonderful secrets!

"Once I get the haul of them—*Lord!*

"I wouldn't do what *he* did; I'd just—well!" He pulls at his pipe.

So he lapses into a dream, the undying, wonderful dream of his life. And though Kemp has fished unceasingly, no human being save the landlord knows those books are there, with the subtle secret of invisibility and a dozen other strange secrets written therein. And none other will know of them until he dies.

BIBLIOGRAPHY

1893   *Text-Book of Biology* (2 vols.).
       Honours Physiography (with R. A. Gregory).
1895   *Select Conversations with an Uncle.*
       The Time Machine.
       The Wonderful Visit.
       The Stolen Bacillus and Other Incidents.
1896   *The Island of Dr. Moreau.*
       The Wheels of Chance.
1897   *The Plattner Story and Others.*
       The Invisible Man.
       Certain Personal Matters.
       Thirty Strange Stories.
1898   *The War of the Worlds.*
1899   *When the Sleeper Wakes.*
       Tales of Space and Time.
1900   *Love and Mr. Lewisham.*
1901   *The First Men in the Moon.*
       Anticipations.
1902   *The Sea Lady.*
1903   *Mankind in the Making.*
       Twelve Stories and a Dream.
1904   *The Food of the Gods.*
1905   *A Modern Utopia.*
       Kipps.
1906   *In the Days of the Comet.*
       The Future in America.
1908   *New Worlds for Old.*
       The War in the Air.

1908   *First and Last Things.*

1909   *Tono Bungay.*
       Anne Veronica.

1910   *The History of Mr. Polly.*

1911   *The New Machiavelli.*
       The Country of the Blind, and Other Stories.
       Floor Games.

1912   *The Great State* (Essays by Wells and 12
           others).
       Marriage.

1913   *Little Wars.*
       The Passionate Friends.

1914   *An Englishman Looks at the World.*
       The World Set Free.
       The Wife of Sir Isaac Harman.

1915   *Boon . . . Being a first selection from the literary
           remains of George Boon . . . with an ambiguous
           introduction by H. G. Wells.*
       Bealby.
       The Research Magnificent.

1916   *What is Coming?*
       Mr. Britling Sees It Through.

1917   *War and the Future.*
       God the Invisible King.
       The Soul of a Bishop.

1918   *In the Fourth Year.*
       Joan and Peter.

1919   *The Undying Fire.*

1920   *The Outline of History* (2 vols.).
       Russia in the Shadows.

1921   *The Salvaging of Civilization.*

1922   *Washington and the Hope of Peace.*
       The Secret Places of the Heart.
       A Short History of the World.

1923 *Men Like Gods.*
The Story of a Great Schoolmaster.
1924 *The Dream.*
A Year of Prophesying.
Atlantic Edition of the Works of H. G. Wells.
(28 vols.).
1925 *A Forecast of the World's Affairs.*
Christina Alberta's Father.
1926 *The World of William Clissold* (3 vols.).
1927 *Meanwhile.*
The Short Stories of H. G. Wells (Benn. Contains a few not previously published).
1928 *The Way the World is going.*
The Open Conspiracy.
Mr. Blessworthy on Rampole Island.
1929 *The King Who Was a King.*
The Adventures of Tommy.
1930 *The Autocracy of Mr. Parham.*
1931 *What are We to Do With Our Lives* (Revised Edition of The Open Conspiracy).
1932 *The Work, Wealth and Happiness of Mankind.*
1933 *The Shape of Things to Come.*
1934 *Experiment in Autobiography.*
1935 *Science of Life* Series with G. P. Wells and Julian Huxley.
Biology of the Human Race.
Drama of Life.
Evolution: Fact and Theory.
History and Advent of Life.
How Animals Behave.
Living Body.
Man's Mind and Behaviour.
Patterns of Life.
Reproduction, Heredity and Development of Sex.

1935 *The New America: the New World.*

1936 *The Anatomy of Frustration: a Modern Synthesis.*

     The Man who could Work Miracles (Film Story).

1937 *Science of Life.*

1938 *World Brain* (Lectures).

     A Propos of Dolores.

     The Brothers.

1939 *The Fate of Homo Sapiens.*

     Brynhild.

     Holy Terror.

1940 *The New World Order.*

     All Aboard for Ararat.

     Babes in the Darkling Wood.

     Film Stories.

     Star Begotten.

     Common Sense of War and Peace (Penguin Special).

1941 *Guide to the New World.*

     A Handbook of Constructive World Revolution.

     You Can't Be Too Careful.

1942 *The Conquest of Time* (Written to replace First and Last Things).

     The Outlook of Homo Sapiens (Amalgamation modernization of The Fate of Homo Sapiens, and The New World Order).

     Phoenix. A Summary of the inescapable conditions of World Reorganisation.

     Science and the World Mind.

1944 *A Contemporary Memoir* (1942-44).

1945 *Mind at the End of its Tether.*

     The Happy Turning.